"Ah, Meg, do you know how hard this is?" Joe groaned

"Yeah, I think I do." Meg pushed seductively against him. "That is, unless you have a gun stuffed down your pants—a rather large-caliber gun, too, I might add," she added, grinning wickedly.

He stared at her, speechless. Then he found his voice. "What I *meant* was, feeling the way I do about you and not being able to act on it...do you know how hard *that* is?"

"So show me," she dared.

Joe's breath caught. "Are you sure, Meg, really? I mean, with everything going on and how crazy it's all been—"

"Joe, I sent out an invitation. Are you telling me no?" She pulled back to look into his eyes.

Joe gave up trying to reason and pressed into her. "What can I say, Meg? It's too *hard* to resist you."

Note from the editor...

An Evening To Remember... Those words evoke all kinds of emotions and memories. How do you plan a romantic evening with your guy that will help you get in touch with each other on every level?

Start with a great dinner that you cook together. Be sure to light several candles and put fresh flowers on the table. Enjoy a few glasses of wine and pick out your favorite music to set the mood. After dinner take the time to really talk to each other. Hold hands and snuggle on the sofa in front of the fireplace. And maybe take a few minutes to read aloud selected sexy scenes from your favorite Harlequin Temptation novel. After that, anything can happen....

That's just one way to have an evening to remember. There are so many more. Write and tell us how you keep the spark in your relationship. And don't forget to check out our Web site at www.eHarlequin.com.

Sincerely,
Birgit Davis-Todd
Executive Editor

CHERYL ANNE PORTER

BLIND DATE

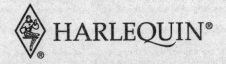

HARLEQUIN®

TORONTO • NEW YORK • LONDON
AMSTERDAM • PARIS • SYDNEY • HAMBURG
STOCKHOLM • ATHENS • TOKYO • MILAN • MADRID
PRAGUE • WARSAW • BUDAPEST • AUCKLAND

To all those women who had to kiss toads until princes finally showed up. Especially the wonderful doctors, nurses and dear friends on my health care team in Tampa, Florida.

ISBN 0-373-69209-9

BLIND DATE

Copyright © 2005 by Cheryl Anne Porter.

All rights reserved. Except for use in any review, the reproduction or utilization of this work in whole or in part in any form by any electronic, mechanical or other means, now known or hereafter invented, including xerography, photocopying and recording, or in any information storage or retrieval system, is forbidden without the written permission of the publisher, Harlequin Enterprises Limited, 225 Duncan Mill Road, Don Mills, Ontario, Canada M3B 3K9.

All characters in this book have no existence outside the imagination of the author and have no relation whatsoever to anyone bearing the same name or names. They are not even distantly inspired by any individual known or unknown to the author, and all incidents are pure invention.

This edition published by arrangement with Harlequin Books S.A.

® and TM are trademarks of the publisher. Trademarks indicated with ® are registered in the United States Patent and Trademark Office, the Canadian Trade Marks Office and in other countries.

www.eHarlequin.com

Printed in U.S.A.

Dear Reader,

On August 25, 2004, wonderfully talented Harlequin Temptation author Cheryl Anne Porter passed away after a valiant struggle with cancer. As her friends, we—the other "Temptresses"—wished to share a few of our fond memories of this vibrant, witty woman.

Without fail, all of us remember laughing with her. Whether because of her outrageous stories, the devilish gleam in her eye, or, as Wendy Etherington remembers, a name tag saying "Queen of the Universe," Cheryl Anne inspired a feeling of genuine happiness from the moment you met her. Carly Phillips recalls meeting Cheryl Anne in a hotel lobby, and says everyone was roaring with laughter within moments of her arrival. Jacquie D'Alessandro distinctly remembers the first time she heard Cheryl's voice—sort of husky, and filled with humor. That warm, softly accented voice was something Leslie Kelly will never forget, as her first interaction with Cheryl Anne was in a phone call.

If you've read Cheryl Anne's books, you probably know her a little yourself. Her voice shone brilliantly through her written words. Julie Kistler was struck by how much Cheryl reminded her of her books, being smart, fresh, genuine and totally original. And Kimberly Raye calls Cheryl one of those people who lives life "out loud," pointing out that, like her books, she made people feel good. Julie Kenner finds comfort that Cheryl's voice, humor and wit will continue to live on through the readers, old and new, who discover her books.

Several of us first met her at writers' conferences, where she was a sought-after speaker. Joanne Rock credits Cheryl Anne with helping her learn to tap deeply into her emotions while writing. Vicki Lewis Thompson fondly recalls the way Cheryl Anne would whip out those pictures of her grandchildren whenever they ran into one another. And every one of us still laughs when we think of Cheryl Anne's "Larry the hotel employee" story.

Jill Shalvis and Julie Elizabeth Leto were fortunate enough to work closely with Cheryl on the MEN OF CHANCE miniseries in Harlequin Temptation, and Jill loved getting to know her. Julie, who lived close to Cheryl Anne, says that on the day Cheryl died, their hometown experienced an awe-inspiring rainstorm that lasted all night—and no one who knew Cheryl was the least surprised that she could influence Mother Nature.

But even those of us who didn't know her personally felt touched by her. Emily McKay is thankful for Cheryl Anne's gifts to the writing community, through her brilliant workshops, her wonderful books and her insightful articles. Rhonda Nelson says that whether you were a good friend, met her but once, or had simply read her wonderful books, the mere thought of Cheryl Anne always evoked a smile.

Finally, Cheryl Anne's editor, Brenda Chin, admits that she's firmly in denial. She's not yet willing to imagine not having the pleasure of collaborating on another book with Cheryl. Cheryl's wit, her irreverence and her outrageousness will be greatly missed by her Harlequin family.

We hope you enjoy this last book by our very dear friend Cheryl Anne Porter. She crafted her stories with love, laughter and genuine emotion...the same way she lived her life. The humor, charm and warmth you're about to experience is her last, personal gift to all of us. One we're all very grateful to have received.

With love,

The Temptresses

Prologue

"OKAY, ON THE COUNT of three, we start taking our clothes off. One—"

"Stop counting! We can't just strip in a department store aisle, Meg!"

"Why not? It'll teach them to put their fitting rooms in obvious locations, won't it?"

Wendy gave her an exasperated look. "Either you quit it right now, or I'm going to call your mother on my cell phone and tell her what you're doing. I don't think the current president of the Women's Garden Club will be amused."

Meg Kendall assessed her best friend for seriousness of intent and decided Wendy Jones would do exactly as she'd threatened. Besides, Meg didn't really intend to follow through with her daring plan. Her conservative upbringing hadn't exactly encouraged wild spontaneity—but it was fun to kid about it. "Oh, all right, you win." Shifting her armload of new spring outfits, Meg again scanned the vicinity for anything resembling a fitting room. "What now, fearless leader? Got any ideas?"

"Yes. We keep looking." Doing just that, Wendy slowly turned around, searching. Suddenly, she pointed off to their left. "Ha. Right over there. See?"

Meg looked where Wendy indicated and saw a subtle but promising doorway cut into a wall of the very upscale department store anchoring one end of Tampa's fabulous International Plaza. She brightened. "Good eye, Wendy."

She set off, weaving her way around several carousels hung with pants and shirts. Mere feet from her destination, Meg was stopped by a restraining hand on her arm. She spun around to face her friend. "Whoa, head rush. What are you doing, Wendy?"

"We can't go in there. These are—" she lowered her voice to a whisper "—the men's fitting rooms." Though equally laden with her own choices in outfits, Wendy managed to point above their heads.

Meg looked up, only now seeing the big blocky letters affixed above the entry. "Oh. So they are. Well, who cares?"

"I do. It's against the law."

"Oh, please. It used to be against the law for women to vote or go braless, but did that stop us? No." Meg again surged forward.

Wendy held her firm. "Men could be in there undressing."

Instant full-color, centerfold-quality snapshots popped into Meg's mind. Hard-bodied athletes and cops and firefighters, all half-naked or better. *Whew.* She shook her head to clear the pictures. "Gorgeous men with their clothes off. How, exactly, is that supposed to dissuade me?"

Wendy released Meg's arm. "What if they look like Maury instead?"

A replacement mental vision of the short, barrel-chested and blustery four-thousand-year-old sweetheart of a little old man who lived in the same complex as she and Wendy did in trendy South Tampa had Meg grimacing her distaste. "Thanks. Now I have to gouge out my mind's eye." She shook her head to clear the image. "Nice try. But I'm still game. I'm tired, my arms are about to fall off from carting these clothes all over the place, and I'm not getting any younger."

"Same here, but first let's think this through…"

"Oh, please, Wendy, not that."

"Just listen. If we go in there, we run the risk of getting caught by the security guards and being charged with a crime, disowned by our families and convicted. If that happens, we'll be sentenced to jail, where, just to survive, we will have to become some big, sweaty chicks' bitches—"

"Big, sweaty— Where *do* you get this stuff?" Meg could hardly believe some of the things that came out of her cute blond, blue-eyed friend's mouth.

"I'm not done. You have to promise me that if we get thrown into jail, we'll pretend to be each other's bitch so no one else will mess with us."

Disbelief rounded Meg's eyes. "You're serious, aren't you."

Wendy nodded. "Go on…promise. I'm waiting."

Knowing from long experience that Wendy would not budge until Meg promised her, she exhaled dramatically. "All right, fine. If we get caught and thrown in jail, I promise we will—and I can't believe I am even going to say this—pretend to be each other's…bitch. There."

"And no farming me out in exchange for cigarettes or chocolate."

"Seriously?" Meg pretended to weigh the pros and cons of such a course of action—Wendy promptly smacked her arm a glancing blow. "Ouch! Okay, fine on the cigarettes. I don't smoke, anyway. But if it comes down to you or chocolate, I'm giving you up, honey."

"That's not funny—"

"Look, if you don't have the guts for this, keep looking for the women's fitting rooms. But don't expect me to wait for you once I've found the dress of my dreams."

Wendy rolled her eyes. "Oh, whatever. But one of these days, I'll figure out why I let you talk me into doing dumb things."

Meg instantly brightened. "It's not dumb, and you do it because you secretly admire my courage."

"Yeah, that's it."

"I know it is." With Wendy once again on her heels, Meg breezed under the forbidden arch. Quickly, she moved down the row of louvered doors, checking to see that each one was indeed empty. For all her bravado, she didn't want to embarrass or alarm some guy. Or go to jail. Or be anybody's bitch.

From behind her, Wendy said, "Back to Maury Seeger, he's quite the character."

Meg couldn't help but warm to the subject of their elderly neighbor. "Maury and his Mafia-mobile," she said, and smiled. Meg could visualize the little old man's hulking, chrome-armored black tank of a car. "I just love Maury and his stories. The way he's always going on about how he was a Mafia don in his younger days and how they called him The Stogie because of his cigars."

"But don't you think Maury—and I mean this in a loving way—has got to have a screw loose? Maybe a whole handful loose?"

Meg shrugged. "Probably. Who doesn't?" Having finished casing the room, she said, "Oh, good, come on—they're all empty." She chose a stall and indicated to Wendy that she should take the one next to hers. Stepping in and closing the door after her, Meg called out, "By the way, did I tell you that I'm going out Saturday night with Maury's great-nephew from out of town?"

"Yeah, you did. That's my point." Wendy's raised voice and the sound of a closing door told Meg her friend had gone into her own fitting room. "This guy is from the same murky gene pool as Maury. Have you thought about that, Meg? And what about Carl? You just broke up with him last weekend. Are you sure that's really over?"

"Beyond sure. Carl's a two-timing jerk. He is *so* out of the picture." Tamping down her simmering anger born of catching Carl out on a date with a woman who definitely had not been her, Meg sorted out the outfits she'd brought with her and hung her choices on the hooks provided. "My evenings are free now, so why shouldn't I go out? Besides, this isn't an actual date. It's a blind date that isn't even really that."

Wendy's voice became teasing instead of scolding. "If it isn't a date, why did it require an evening trek to the mall in the middle of the week to buy a new outfit?"

"It didn't. We came for you. You're the one looking for something to wear on the airplane Friday afternoon." Meg tossed her purse down and unsnapped her lightweight denim dress. "I just got lucky and found some cool things I like. Anyway, what's the harm in wanting to make a good first impression?"

"I knew it! Tell me again how this isn't a date, blind or otherwise?"

"It's not. It's a favor." Meg considered her first selection. A scarlet linen shift, the hem of which was encircled with tiny rows of multicolored chain-stitch embroidery. A definite possibility. "I'm doing a nice thing for a little old man who owns a spot in my heart. His nephew is coming and he asked me if I'd just show the guy around Tampa for one evening. Big deal. So I'll give him the three-hour tour." Standing in her bra and panties, Meg unzipped the linen dress and stepped into it.

"Meg, you do realize, don't you, that this guy could be a serial killer?"

Meg settled the dress on herself and performed all the standard contortions a woman does to get a zipper up. "It's not like I picked up some ax-wielding, smelly psycho from the side of the road. The guy's a foreman for a construction company in Colorado." She admired herself in the mirror. The dress fit perfectly. "Are you having any luck over there? I am totally loving this red linen dress."

"Really? I'm not too sure about this blue suit. I like it, but if I'm going to wear it on my trip, I want it to be comfortable. Maybe I need the next larger size," she said with a sigh.

The sound of an opening door told Meg that Wendy had just exited her fitting room. "Wait here for me, okay? I'm dressed and I have my purse. I'm going to go look for that next size."

"All right," Meg said. She reached around behind her to undo the zipper and about four or five inches from the bottom, the zipper balked…and then stuck.

Meg felt for the snag, found it and grimaced. *Great.* It was stuck on the lace at the top of her bikini underwear. And no matter how she fiddled with it, it would not come loose. *Damn it.* Short of pulling the dress down and off—along with her underwear, which would leave her naked from the waist down— Meg was doomed to stand there, frustrated. Where was Wendy when she needed her?

At that exact moment, the door to the next stall closed. Wendy was back! Meg opened her stall's door, went to the next one and knocked on it. "Hey, before you take your clothes off, would you get this stupid zipper unstuck for me? It's caught in my underwear."

STANDING IN THE MEN'S fitting room stall, already shirtless but still in his jeans, Joe Rossi didn't budge as his mind processed what he'd just heard. A knock on his door. A female voice. A zipper stuck in her underwear. And she wanted his help.

That didn't happen every day.

But what the hell was she doing in here? Was she mistaking him for a boyfriend or husband? Probably. So this would be funny when she saw him and realized her mistake. Unable to resist his impulse to play this scene out, Joe opened the door, ready to see the surprise on her face and laugh with her.

Only, she wasn't facing him. She had her back to him and her hands pinched in at her waist to keep the dress's two back panels loose. Her head was bent forward, which sent cascades of shiny brunette hair falling forward over her shoulders. Joe swallowed. If her front was even half as nice as her back, then this was one really hot woman. She stood about average height, had a great figure—the parts he could see—and lightly tanned skin. Her bra was white and lacy. Her dress was open to below her waist. And, sure enough, the zipper was caught on her underwear.

Joe was torn. He wished he could help her out, but not for all the money in country music was he going to touch her. Not that he didn't want to. He'd be pleased to. But he didn't dare, not without informed consent, which this scenario did not imply—

"Sweetie, what are you doing back there? See if you can get the zipper unstuck. I don't want to have to take off the dress, and my underwear along with it, so I can work on it myself. How embarrassing would *that* be?"

"More so for you than me," Joe said.

The woman tensed, her head came up, and she apparently stared straight ahead. Suddenly, she swung around, her eyes wide, her hands covering her mouth as she stared at him in shock.

"Don't scream." Joe already had his hands out in front of him in a stop-right-there gesture. "It's okay. I'm not going to hurt you—"

She moved her hands about an inch away from her mouth. "You don't have on a shirt."

"You're absolutely right. I do not have on a shirt." A lucid corner of his brain—one not involved in this debacle—noted that her front was every bit as hot as her back. This woman smoldered. Wide brown eyes. Bedroom eyes. He flicked his gaze over her fine nose, down to her sensual, rosy lips, then her slender neck, to her full set of breasts—and right back up to her eyes. "I had just pulled off my shirt and was getting ready to try one on when you knocked on the door. I can show it to you if you like. The shirt, I mean."

"No. Not necessary. I believe you." She sounded breathless, apologetic. "I am so embarrassed. I thought you were someone else." She tucked a stray lock of her thick, shiny, reddish brown hair behind her ear. "She was here a minute ago, I swear."

"She?" Joe's interest level ratcheted up significantly—a purely male response to a hot, possibly unattached and half-dressed woman.

"Yes. My friend Wendy," the woman said distractedly as she blatantly checked him out. "Okay, I just have to say something, and it's very politically incorrect. But all of this—" she waved her hand up and down him, indicating his bare chest "—*wow*. On the other hand, I am so sorry. How uncool am I? I've never even seen you before, and I just stick my booty right in your face."

"Well, it wasn't exactly…in my face." Still, Joe's testosterone-soaked brain created some really nice images of that. *Really nice*. But he probably shouldn't linger there. *Say something*. "What, exactly, are you doing in the men's fitting rooms, anyway?"

Wrinkling her nose, which only made her cuter, she sighed. "It's a long story that involves women in line scratching and shoving, and I don't come off very well in it. So, really, it's not worth retelling." She backed up a step and, hands behind her, clutched at her dress. "Anyway, I should just…go. Again, sorry. I really did think you were my friend."

Though acutely aware that he shouldn't say what

he was thinking, given his situation with Linda, his would-be fiancée, Joe nevertheless shrugged. "I could be your friend, if you wanted me to be."

Awareness flared in her eyes, but then she chuckled and shook her head. "I'm sorry, but a guy like you? If all you wanted to be was my friend, I'd have to kill myself."

Amused and self-conscious, Joe swept his gaze down and away before recovering enough to face her again. When he did, he was trapped. He couldn't look away from those mesmerizing brown eyes. "So…what do we do now?"

"Do?" She raised her eyebrows. "*We* don't do anything. In fact, we pretty much never see each other again because this is the most embarrassing moment of my life."

A stab of disappointment surprised Joe. "Are you sure?"

She frowned. "Well, unless we count that time in high school when my swimsuit bra came up as I jumped off the high dive—"

"No, I mean, are you sure that we can never see each other again?" He couldn't believe he'd said that. He had no right. And yet, here he was flirting—and maybe wanting this chance encounter to go somewhere.

"Oh God," she said, covering her face with her hands again, but not before he saw her turning red. "First I talk about my butt and then my boobs." She was talking through the web of her overlapping fingers. "Can you just go back in that fitting room and forget about all this? Just pretend you never saw me and that this didn't happen?"

His voice ringing with as much regret as humor,

Joe said, "Sure. I can go back in the fitting room. But I have to tell you, it will be damned hard to forget this ever happened."

1

"It's FRIDAY EVENING, Meg," she said to herself, "you're alone in your apartment, your date tonight is with a department store, and—wait for it—you're talking to yourself. How sad is that?" She grabbed up her handbag, turned the light off in her spacious bedroom, and walked down the narrow, carpeted hallway toward the living room. At least she lived in a great place. The Mediterranean-style courtyard apartment complex, with over two hundred units, was *the* address for young singles in Tampa. "Okay, so maybe I'm not totally pathetic."

At least she looked good, dressed in her new V-neck, white T-shirt and stretchy, hip-hugging khaki pants. She wished Wendy could see her in them, but her friend had left today for a wedding in Dallas. On the other hand, school was out for spring break. *Finally.* That meant no precious little third-graders to teach for a whole week. *Bless their hearts.* And tomorrow night she had a date-that-wasn't-a-date. A date who also wasn't Carl "the high school football coach and big, fat cheater" Woodruff. So, life was good.

However, it would be even better if, instead of going out with Maury's great-nephew tomorrow, she'd see Mr. Hot and Shirtless from the dressing room debacle two evenings ago. That man was causing her to toss and turn at night with torrid dreams of anonymous sex in a fitting room. Meg felt the tightening of desire tense her tummy muscles. "Great. One look from the guy in the tight jeans and the oh-my-God chest and I'm signing up for sex with him in elevators, airplanes and swimming pools."

Sighing over what could not be, Meg sorted through her designated junk drawer in the tiny wet bar in her living room. Spying what she was looking for, she grabbed up the small can of pepper spray—blame Wendy's talk of serial killers—and dropped the defensive weapon into her purse. "Wait. Car keys." Rooting through her purse for those, Meg grimaced in sympathy for Wendy, who was at her younger sister's wedding. "Younger. That hurts."

It didn't especially fill Meg with joy, either. Here she was, already twenty-five—practically middle-aged—and she had yet to fire some guy's jets to the point of a white dress and ring.

Meg found her keys and zipped her purse closed, wishing she could do the same thing with her bridal and hormonal thoughts. Apparently there was nothing like a wedding to make a woman rethink her whole love life. "What love life?" She checked her wristwatch. "Yikes. Nearly seven. Time to shop."

Holding her purse by its straps, like a bunny by the ears, Meg made for the sofa, where earlier, she'd stashed the department-store bag that held the new red dress she intended to return. Somehow, it hadn't looked quite as stunning at home. As she reached for the bag, though, she caught her reflection in the large, framed mirror behind the sofa. Straightening, she checked out her "studied casual" look. After all, a girl never knew who else might be at the mall on a Friday evening. Like maybe some exciting man exchanging a shirt he'd just bought?

Meg turned this way and that checking her makeup…her teeth…her outfit. She fluffed her hair—and stared in shock. "When did my hair start sticking out on the sides like that?"

She tossed her keys and purse onto the sofa, tucked her long, layered hair behind her ears and checked out the effect. "Sucks." She freed her hair and ran her fingers through it, muttering, "It's not my hair. It's my ears. Dad's ears. God, I could fly with these things, like Dumbo—"

The phone rang, cutting off her words. It was probably Mom, who had telepathically heard her daughter say something mean about her bank president father's ears. Meg reached over to the end table to retrieve the phone and hit the talk button. "Hello."

The voice at the other end of the line—definitely not her mother's—raised Meg's hackles and reminded her she really needed to get caller ID. "Hello, Carl. What do you want?"

She listened for a moment, and decided that was all she could take. "You know what Carl? It's a little late to say you miss me. What happened to your other *friend?* You know, the one you had that nice little date with the other night? Yes, I am still mad. And no, I don't think I'll forgive you. In fact, I don't even want to talk to you…." She paused for a minute, waiting for it to sink in. It didn't. "No, Carl, you can't come over and discuss this with me," she said, trying again. "There's nothing to talk about. Besides, I have plans."

Shopping by one's self could certainly be called plans. "No, Carl. Do not come over. I will not be here. I swear I won't. What? Yes, you actually are that easy to get over. Shocking, isn't it? Oh, but I do mean it— I'm over you. No, I won't be here. Do not come over. And now I'm hanging up. Goodbye."

Though she could still hear him talking, Meg angrily pressed the end button and plunked the phone back onto its base. "Take that, you cheating—"

An abrupt knocking on her front door cut off her unflattering sentiment. Instinctively, she headed for the door but stopped after one step and stood there, thinking. She looked at the phone and then the door. Could Carl have been standing right outside when he called on his cell phone? A cutesy trick like that was just like him, she decided, now striding stiffly toward her entryway. "Well, I'll give him an earful he won't soon forget. A real tongue-lashing, by God. And not the good kind, either."

Muttering, her anger building, she stepped onto the tile squares of the minuscule entryway. Why it couldn't be the nice, gorgeous, shirtless guy from the department store standing on the other side of the door when she opened it, she'd never know. Talk about your six feet of hunk with blue eyes and sandy-brown hair. *Yeah, right. In my dreams. But who do I get? Stupid Carl and his little cell-phone trick.*

Meg twisted the dead bolt and jerked the door open, already talking as it swung wider. "Look, I don't think you're one bit funny. I told you not to come over here, you big—" She came to an embarrassed stop as her disbelieving eyes and brain got together and made the connection. This wasn't Carl.

"Oh my God, I thought you were someone else—again!" she cried out. "What are you doing here?"

The six-foot hunk from the fitting room incident stared at her in shock. "You!"

"I know!" This was just too bizarre, and Meg's mind wouldn't process it. Feeling weak, as if she might faint, she jerked back and slammed the door in his face.

"No, don't—" Too late. Joe knocked hard on the freshly slammed door. "Hey, are you okay in there?" He waited. No answer. *Well, now what?* He stood in the breezeway, feeling the warm evening air wash over him. "Hello!" he called out again, concerned. "Are you all right?"

While he worried, another part of his brain worked on the fact that it was *her*—the really hot woman from the dressing room. Man, she certainly hadn't lost anything in the translation. But this couldn't be right. Hell, if he played these odds in Vegas, he'd own the town.

Looking for help, Joe turned around and peered over the iron railing to the pool, four floors below. He glanced at the lush, tropical landscaping with its lighted walkway meandering through the generous grounds and the park benches set at intervals throughout. There wasn't a soul in sight. He turned to the door again and knocked. "Listen, if you don't answer me right now, I'm going to get the manager to open this door. So if you can hear me—"

"I can hear you" came a muffled voice from the other side of the closed door. "And I'm all right. I just wasn't expecting you to be here. I thought you were stupid Carl."

Joe weighed that for significance. "Carl must have really messed up."

"Oh, he did. Big time."

Acutely conscious of how their semi-shouting match might appear to the neighbors, Joe stepped in closer and said, "Look, I think I can explain this if you'll just open the door. You already know I'm not Carl, and I swear I'm not a stalker. Maury Seeger sent me."

A moment of silence ensued. "Are you a hit man?"

Uncle Maury had obviously been spreading his Mafia stories. "No."

"Would you tell me if you were?"

"Probably not. But, look, think about it for a minute. Didn't Maury tell you to expect a visitor, one who isn't a hit man?"

"Yes and no. What's your name and where do you live?"

This was a test. "Joe Rossi, and I live in Denver."

"What do you do there?"

"I'm a construction foreman."

"Okay, what's my name? And, yes, I know what it is. I want to see if you do."

"I figured." He extracted a piece of paper from his pants pocket and consulted it. "Meg Kendall?"

"Right. So, what are you doing here, Joe Rossi?"

"We have a date at seven."

The door opened and the sexy brunette stood there, frowning. "We do not. It's tomorrow night. And it's not really a date. It's just an outing. So to speak."

"No, it's tonight…whatever it is." He could not get enough of looking at her. She just oozed an appealing mix of humor and sleepy sensuality…like a lazy Sunday afternoon spent in bed teasing and laughing and making love. Joe exhaled loudly. "Are you all right? I mean, you looked so shocked a minute ago—"

"Yeah, I'm okay. It was just such a surprise. But our…*outing* is still tomorrow night."

Just as she had in the fitting room, she roved her gaze up and down his length, making Joe feel like a stud in the show ring. Far from offended, he had all he could do not to strike a manly weightlifting pose and flex his biceps for her. "And yet, here I am. Tonight."

"I noticed. And *you're* Maury Seeger's nephew? Really?"

"No. I'm his great-nephew. My grandmother was his late wife's sister."

Still holding onto the doorknob, she said, "Sounds complicated."

"What hasn't been so far?"

"True. But just so you know—" she narrowed her eyes and crossed her arms "—I have pepper spray in my purse, and I'm not afraid to use it."

That slowed Joe down for a second. "Okay. But you should know I carry a small Swiss Army knife, most of the functions of which I have no idea."

While she digested that, Joe flicked his gaze up and down her, deciding she looked damn nice in pants. Long legs. She also filled out her T-shirt admirably. And her hair looked like she'd just climbed out of bed…and not in a bad way, either.

Because the silence between them was getting long and awkward, Joe said, "Tried on any good clothes lately?"

Her expression crumpled in amused embarrassment. "I cannot believe I did that. I am still absolutely mortified."

Instantly charmed, Joe grinned. "It wasn't all that bad, was it?"

She wagged a scolding finger at him. "Yes, it was. And I told you we couldn't ever see each other again."

"I don't remember agreeing to that."

"True. But then you have to promise you will not, under any circumstances, ever bring up that incident again."

Still feeling devilish, and pretty sure she could take a joke when it was on her, Joe replied, "You mean the part where you were half-naked in the men's fitting rooms and poked your booty in my face?"

Crying out, she slapped at his arm—and missed because he danced back just in time. "I said don't bring it up."

Joe held up both hands in surrender. "Okay, it's in the vault. I swear."

"Good." She relaxed enough to lean against the doorjamb and again cross her arms under her excellent breasts. He wished like hell she'd quit doing that and drawing his attention there. Or maybe he didn't. "Seriously, what are you doing here tonight?" she said, drawing his attention back to her face. "Maury told me Saturday night."

"And he told me tonight. He gets things wrong sometimes."

Her expression radiated fond affection. "I know. But he's such a sweet little man. Other than that, I don't know what to say, Joe. I can't really show you around Tampa tonight." She turned just enough to look back inside her apartment before facing him again. "Or maybe I can. Or should. I don't know. I don't want to be here if…"

"Are we talking about Carl?"

She wrinkled her nose as if the man's name smelled bad. "Yes. I told him not to come over, that I had plans—"

"Which didn't include me."

"Right. I have to return a dress. Which means I don't have anything to wear right now. And that means we can't go out tonight."

Joe made it a rule never to try to understand or argue with feminine logic. Still, he stopped short of saying that she could go naked, for all he cared. "Well, if it makes any difference, you look great to me just as you are."

She glanced down at herself. "I don't know. I was going to wear—I mean tomorrow night—this little red, sleeveless linen sheath with tiny rows of embroidered stitching all around the hem that I bought. But then I decided I didn't really like it and should take it back—" She cut off her own words. "You don't care, do you."

Joe shook his head apologetically. "It's not that I don't care. It's just that, like most men, I'm genetically programmed to understand only football rules and beer commercials. All I heard of what you said was la-la-la-linen, la-la-la-stitching."

She laughed. "You poor Neanderthal. It's lonely out there in the cave, isn't it."

"It is. And it's cold. But we have great hopes for something called fire."

Certain they were now on better footing, Joe

added, "So, here's a plan. We go out tonight *and* tomorrow night. That way, neither one of us has it wrong. Or has to admit it. Or will be here should Carl show up."

"He'd better not." But still, she stood there as she looked up at him with those big, brown bedroom eyes.

"So, what's Colorado like? Lots of cowboys and snowmobiles?"

All right, she was still undecided and this was a stall tactic. Joe wondered, though, if she felt the same subtle force he did, the one that urged him to step closer to her. "Let's see…Colorado. Well, it's rocky, like you'd expect. Mountainous. Trees everywhere. And cold. Lots of snow. A few cowboys. Now it's your turn. Where are you from? Uncle Maury didn't tell me much about you, except that you are beautiful and have a great personality."

A tinge of pink stained her cheeks as she shook her head. "Maury exaggerates."

"Not in this case."

"And now you're just being nice. I'm a native Floridian, from Gainesville, where my family still lives. And I teach third grade."

"Gainesville, huh? Go 'Gators. But third grade? Suddenly, I understand your need for pepper spray."

Again she laughed. "They're not as bad as all that. But their parents…" A dramatic roll of her eyes completed her joke.

Joe didn't know what to say next, so he just stood there grinning and nodding—like an idiot, he feared. An awkward silence fell over them and slowly became painful.

"So," he said abruptly, causing Meg to blink, "is

this the actual date? The two of us standing here, you inside, me outside, talking?"

"Oh. No. Sorry." She stepped aside and gestured for him to enter. "It's not a date, but come in."

He took a step forward.

"Or should I just get my purse?"

Joe stopped, waiting for her to decide.

"No, come in."

Joe started forward again.

"Oh, darn, I still need to return that dress to the store, and I was on my way out when you knocked."

Wanting to forestall any further doorway do-si-do, Joe suggested, "Why don't we just return the dress when we're out on our not-a-date?"

She brightened, smiling. "You wouldn't mind? Really? Or maybe I should just wear the new dress."

Joe thought he had her figured out well enough by now to say, "But you hate the new dress. And don't go change clothes. You look fine to me in what you have on. Besides, I don't have any big, fancy plans for this evening."

"You don't? Why not?"

Clearly she meant, *Am I not worth it?*

Joe thought fast. "I just meant it's your town, Meg. I thought I'd be ready for anything you might want to do. That's why I dressed like this." He indicated his casual attire—jeans, neatly belted, and maroon knit shirt.

That seemed to satisfy her. "Okay. I was going to suggest dinner and then I'd show you the city…but tomorrow night, so I'm kind of disappointed."

"I still don't understand why we can't do it tonight."

"Because the free concert at Centro Ybor isn't until tomorrow."

"Yeah, that makes it hard." Joe's frown was for the unfamiliar term. "What's Centro Ee-bore? Where's that?"

Her expression brightened. "Oh, it's fun. All kinds of stores, restaurants and clubs, and even a movie complex. It's close by, just the other side of the Crosstown Expressway in Y-B-O-R City. Anyway, it's the Latin Quarter of Tampa. Really historic. All about Cuban cigars. You'd like it."

"Sounds like I would. We could still go tomorrow night…if you want. If we still like each other."

"If we still do? So you think we like each other now?" Flirtatious best described her crooked grin.

It had an immediate—and elevating—effect on Joe. He stuffed his hands in his pants pockets to keep from grabbing her and kissing the hell out of her. Man, he just kept digging this hole of attraction deeper and deeper, didn't he. Sure, he'd come here to visit his favorite relative, but also to take time away to think about his relationship with Linda, a really fine woman he'd been with now for about six months. She wanted things to get more serious…but he didn't. So these ten days in Florida—three of which had already passed—were his chance to decide what he should do.

"You're awfully quiet, cowboy. I mean, if you have to think about it that long, then—"

"Sorry." Snapped back to the moment, Joe pulled his hands out of his pants pockets. *Cowboy?* Gazing at Meg Kendall's pretty face, he decided he liked her teasing reference to his home state. This woman was going to keep him on his toes, he could just tell. "Yeah, we do. We like each other."

Her attractive grin widened considerably. "Cool."

Feeling way too warm, even for Tampa's temperate evening air, Joe searched for something neutral to say. "We'll be taking Uncle Maury's car. You still want to go?"

She made a face. "Yes, but we can take my car, if you want."

Smiling, Joe said, "So you've experienced the black and chrome monster. Personally, I would love to take your car, but we'd better take his. Evidently, he spent a whole week before I got here cleaning and polishing it. He's pretty proud of it, and I'd hate to hurt his feelings."

"Aren't you a good nephew."

Embarrassed, Joe feigned immediate insult. "Now, don't go around saying things like that. If you ruin my reputation as the tough guy, cowboy type, I'd have to beat someone up all over again."

"Really? Because there's a guy named Carl I'd like to nominate for that honor. He's kind of big, but I think you could take him."

"Ah, yes…Carl. What did he do, exactly?" Joe couldn't believe how much he enjoyed just standing here talking to her. Who cared if they went anywhere?

"Carl was a jerk, that's what," Meg said.

"Well, then, we don't like him." He gestured toward the door. "So, are you ready? Uncle Maury is bringing his car around from the parking garage. Once we're on our way—with everyone in Tampa staring at us—we'll go find this Carl and I'll take care of him for you. How's that sound for a start to a nice evening?"

Meg grinned. "I'll go get my purse."

"And the dress."

"Right. And the dress."

2

"So, how about this little beauty, huh, Joey? It's part of my legacy. When I die, it's all yours."

"You're not going to die, Uncle Maury. The way things are going, you'll be around longer than I am. You and this…car." Standing in the apartment complex's parking lot with Meg at his side, Joe looked over the black and chrome behemoth that could have been a prop in a James Cagney gangster movie. But his great-uncle was so proud of the car that Joe had no choice but to voice excitement. "Still looks like it's in mint condition."

"It's better than that. Got a new engine. And I put new tires on it and installed seat belts. It's gassed up, street-legal and ready to go." Wearing striped and rumpled shorts, a loud Hawaiian shirt and scuffed deck shoes, the short, stocky, cigar-smoking and toupee-topped octogenarian indulgently patted the car's fender. "This baby saw me through many a scrape up in Jersey in the old days. What a machine. It's not the same now—the cars and the gangsters today. They don't have anything on us old guys. We were the real deal—you know, kid?"

"Yes, I do, Uncle Maury." As an aside to Meg, Joe

whispered, "He was never in the Mafia. Not really. I'll tell you more later."

"Okay," she whispered back, "but I didn't really think he was."

"Before I got out of the mob," Maury continued, "we were really something. But these goons today, all dressed in black, so slick and educated? Hooey! A bunch of empty suits. Got no morals. No respect." He wagged a stubby index finger at Joe. "A man who don't respect his family is no kind of man at all. You remember that, Joey. And you take good care of my little Meggie here. She's a gem, ain't she?"

Maury cupped her chin in his hand and grinned proudly. "Beautiful, like I told you, huh? She teaches little kids. Tells them what they need to know about life—don't you, Meggie?"

"I try, Maury." Her voice sounded funny since she had to speak with her cheeks pooched between his big thumb and thick fingers.

Maury released her, leaving red marks on her face. Joe didn't know what to do or say as she worked her jaw, but she she acted like this was an everyday occurrence that didn't upset her.

"That's my girl." Maury dug through his pockets, obviously searching for something. "You need any money, Joey, to show this lady a good time? She deserves some fun."

"I've got plenty, Uncle Maury. Keep your money." But Maury pressed a big wad of bills into Joe's hand anyway. "Well, in that case, thank you. That's really nice of you." He tucked the money into his pocket. It was just easier. Tomorrow he'd find a way to put it back on his uncle's dresser. The top of it was such a mess he'd never notice a few loose dollars added back to the mix.

"Hey," Meg said suddenly. "Why don't you come with us, Maury?"

That surprised Joe. Sure it was nice that she'd want to include the old guy. But did she offer because she didn't want to be alone with him?

Uncle Maury, God love him, came through. With broad gestures and an adamant shake of his head that left his toupee slightly askew, he waved Meg's suggestion away. "No, you two go. You don't want an old man tagging along. Go enjoy a little adventure. Maybe tomorrow when I'm not so tired, we can do something, the three of us. How does that sound?"

With the words no more than said, Maury was suddenly seized with an episode of coughing and wheezing that had him clutching at his chest.

Concerned, Joe took up position beside his uncle. At the same time, Meg took his elbow at the other side. Really liking this woman for her warmth and caring, Joe turned his attention to Maury. "You're tired? Are you all right?"

"I'm fine," he groused, shaking off their hands.

Joe stepped back, exchanging a look with Meg, who looked every bit as worried as he felt. The old guy might be a kid at heart, but Joe had to remind himself that his great-uncle was well into his eighties. "Why don't we just stay here with you tonight, Uncle Maury?"

Seeking her approval, Joe again met Meg's eyes and saw her nod. "We'll call out for a pizza and you can tell us all about the old days. How does that sound?"

"Boring as hell. You go paint the town with the young lady. Me, I got some people coming over tonight. We'll sit by the pool, have a few drinks, play some cards and tell lies. I'll be fine. Now, go. Get outta here."

Joe frowned, suddenly worried about leaving Maury alone. Maybe moving from the active-seniors complex where he used to live hadn't been such a good idea for his great-uncle. The family had taken it as a good sign when Maury left last year, saying he didn't want to be surrounded by old people. Now, Joe wasn't so sure.

"Why the long face, Joey?" Maury chided. "I said I was fine. Now, you kids go have fun. And make sure Meggie here cuts loose a little, Joey. But be a gentleman, or you'll answer to me."

Joe held his hands up in mock surrender. "Okay, okay. We'll go, and I'll behave."

"Darn, Maury, why'd you have to make him promise to behave?" Meg pouted, clamping her hands to her waist. "Are you just trying to take all the fun out of this evening?"

Meg's teasing sentiment—though Joe suspected she'd said it mainly to make Uncle Maury laugh, which he did—nevertheless riveted Joe's attention on her. She boldly met his gaze, but only for an instant before she leaned in to kiss his elderly great-uncle on the cheek. Watching her, Joe again had the sense, deep inside, that she was not going to be an easy woman to walk away from.

A LITTLE MORE THAN three hours into their not-a-date, as they motored down stately Bayshore Boulevard with the un-air-conditioned jalopy's front windows rolled down, Meg found herself looking over at Joe. Though he was seat-belted in behind the wheel of the Mafia-mobile, he wasn't all that far away. For all its chrome and length, the car's interior was fairly compact. No more than a foot of empty bench seat separated her from this fine specimen of maleness.

"How long have you been here visiting Maury?" she asked, deciding a little conversation might break the ice.

"Three days now."

"Really? I'm surprised I haven't seen you around the apartment complex." Meg loved that Joe was driving. This way she could look at him all she wanted, without worrying about where they were going. The man had a killer face—high forehead and cheekbones, deep-set blue eyes, a straight nose, sensual lips and a firm jaw. He looked like a tough-guy movie star. But most of all, she liked how a lock of his sandy hair, which looked darker in the night, fell over his forehead. "Where have you been—camped out by the pool so you could check out all the bikini babes?"

"Only for about the first twenty-four hours." He grinned over at her, showing beautiful white teeth, then returned his attention to the traffic. "I was wondering why I hadn't seen you, either. But I guess it's because Uncle Maury's place is so far away from yours. You've got a whole other entrance and street address."

"Yes, the stinker has the best apartment in the complex. But I was at work all this last week. And except for Wednesday evening when I went shopping—as you well know but aren't allowed to talk about—I was home grading papers. Anyway, all I can say is thank God this upcoming week is our spring break."

Looking really pleased, Joe nodded. "It is? So you're off all week?"

If he was happy about that, then so was she. A heat deep in her abdomen grew at the spark of awareness she saw in his eyes. "Yes, I am."

"And you're not going anywhere?"

Meg raised her eyebrows. "Are you trying to get rid of me?"

"Hardly. I was just thinking that this is Florida, spring-break mecca. I figured you'd join the festivities, like in all those old beach movies."

"Not me. I grew up doing that. All the drinking, sleeping around, getting thrown in jail…it gets old pretty fast." Enjoying the shocked disbelief on his face, Meg confessed. "I was just kidding. I didn't do those things. Well, not all of them."

"Imagine my disappointment."

"Ha-ha. So, how long are you staying?"

"Another week." Joe's blue eyes glittered black in the semidarkness. "Pretty good timing on my part, huh?"

Meg playfully turned up her nose at him. "Don't be so sure of yourself. I never said I'd spend the whole week with you."

She wished like crazy she had the nerve to undo her seat belt, scoot over next to him and put her hand on his rock-solid leg as they rode along. And maybe he'd put his muscular arm around her. And they'd be like something out of *Grease*—hopefully, an R-rated *Grease*.

"So, where to now, Meg? We've returned your dress, eaten at that cheesecake place, talked about our families and our entire lives up to now, seen the former Tampa Bay Hotel along the Hillsborough River, which now houses the University of Tampa—" he grinned over at her "—not the river, the former hotel. See? I was paying attention on the tour."

Meg nodded. "You better be, cowboy. I don't do this for everyone."

"Good. That means I'm special. So, what do we do next?"

We climb in the back seat and make out. Startled, Meg blinked, perfectly ready to get out and walk, if she'd said that out loud. But with his face lit by the passing streetlights and headlamps of other cars, Joe was merely dividing his attention between the road and her, an air of innocent expectancy on his face. *Thank God.* "Okay, let's see. Oh, I know. We could get a drink on Harbour Island. There's a really nice open-air bar there with live music. Jazz. A very *in* place to be."

Joe nodded. "Sounds like fun. But I was thinking maybe we should park somewhere and make out hot and heavy."

His voice was teasing but it had a deep, sensual undertone that sent shivers up her spine.

"This car just seems to beg for that—doesn't it?" he added.

Shocked, Meg gulped, unable to speak.

"And there it is—the fish-out-of-water response." Joe's lip curled into an engaging Elvis Presley grin. "Sorry. I shouldn't have said that, should I?"

Meg fought to catch her breath. "It's not that. You just surprised me. Only a minute ago I was going

to…well, I was going to suggest the same thing…"
A flash of something electric in his eyes nearly lit the
car's interior. "Really?"

Meg nodded. "Really."

Apparently, that was enough for Joe. "I'm going
to change lanes and find a place to pull over."

A thrill of dangerous excitement coursed through
Meg. Maybe she shouldn't have started this. Could
she finish it? Joe was a hottie, no doubt about that,
and she'd all but wished him to be at her door earlier and, yes, she'd had all those sexy thoughts about
him, all that was true. But this was getting pretty
darned real way too fast. After all, he was here only
for a week. That had *casual fling* written all over it. Before she could totally dismiss that idea, Meg's libido
seized it, telling her maybe that was exactly what
she needed right now.

She eyed Joe openly, finally concluding she
couldn't think of any man she'd rather be flung by
than him. "So, once you pull over, Joe, what exactly
do you intend to do?"

"Something I've been wanting to do since I first
saw you."

"Oh God, I ate onions." Now, why had she said
that? *Why?* Meg almost groaned at how uncool she'd
sounded.

Joe shrugged. "Won't bother me. So did I. Hang
on," he said as he turned the wheel.

Meg wondered if she could dig through her purse,
find her mints, pop one into her mouth and hurriedly
suck the good out of it—without Joe realizing it. No,
that wouldn't work. Well, maybe he wouldn't be able
to pull over and park. After all, changing lanes—

much less pulling over—on Bayshore wouldn't be that easy. The four-lane avenue, lined with million-dollar mansions on one side of the grassy median and the waters of Tampa Bay on the other, was busy with a steady stream of Friday-evening revelers.

But she hadn't counted on Joe's determination. He expertly pulled the unwieldy cruiser into the right lane and, within the next half mile, found the one public parking area on the water's side.

Joe cut the motor, undid his seat belt and turned toward her. "Meg Kendall, I've been wanting to do this since I first saw you with that zipper stuck in your panties."

Though Meg's heart thumped like a bass drum and she could barely swallow, she managed to choke out, "You said you wouldn't bring that up again."

Joe reached for her and, tenderly gripping her arm, slowly pulled her toward him. "I lied. That scene is all I think about at night." His voice, low and husky, had her breathing through her open mouth. "How you looked standing there with your back to me. The curve of your spine. How soft your skin looked. And how much I wanted you."

Oh God. Her bones were melting right along with her resistance and her no-sex-on-the-first-date rule. Meg allowed herself to be tugged toward him.

By the time Joe had her in his arms, Meg could no longer form coherent thoughts. She had one hand on his forearm, the skin warm and firm, and the other against his chest...no less firm and warm even through his knit shirt. His languid blue eyes still looked black in the night. Joe slowly slipped his hand up under her hair and around the back of her neck.

Such a simple gesture, yet so incredibly erotically charged.

"I'm going to kiss you, Meg."

"And I'm going to kiss you right back, Joe." Meg moved in toward him, tipping her head to one side and parting her lips. Joe dipped his head down to hers. His lips were a mere inch from hers—

A cell phone rang stridently.

Meg jumped back, and so did Joe. The sexy-as-hell man slumped back against the seat and muttered a soft "Damn."

Chagrined, Meg plucked her purse off the floor and unzipped it. "I cannot believe this. Is it mine or yours?"

Joe stretched up off the seat and pulled his phone off the clip attached to his belt. He stared at it. "It's not mine."

"I am so sorry." Sure enough, she pulled a ringing phone out of her purse. "I have no idea who this can be. I should have turned the stupid thing off. In fact, why don't I just do that now?"

Joe held up a hand to stop her. "No. Take the call. It's probably a good thing someone called, considering where we were headed just now."

Meg stared at him.

So he was already having second thoughts about that kiss. Disappointed, she hit the answer button and put the obtrusive little instrument to her ear. "Hello."

The answering voice put her right over the edge. She looked over at Joe and mouthed *It's Carl.* He nodded and watched her. Not breaking eye contact with the delicious man sitting next to her in the car, Meg dealt with her caller. "This isn't a good time, Carl. Yes, I know I'm not home. I told you I was going out—Wait a minute. Are you there at my place right now?"

Next to her, Joe sat up tensely. He looked ready to start the car, drive back to the apartment complex and beat the hell out of Carl. Meg figured she'd better hurry her cheating ex-boyfriend off the phone. Much as she'd like to see him pounded to a pulp, she didn't want Joe charged with assault. "Well, you better not be there. Anyway, we don't really have anything to say to each other. What? It's none of your business who I'm with, or if I'm even with anyone."

What Carl next said into her ear stopped Meg for a good two to three seconds and had her pulse tripping. "What? No, you can't say that now. It's too late to tell me you love me. Just forget— *Marry you?* You want me to *marry you?*"

Joe abruptly turned away from her and stared out the window to his left. Her mind reeling, Meg didn't know what to do, what to say. Joe—perhaps thinking she wanted privacy for this conversation—opened the car door and got out, closing it behind him.

Meg had reached out to stop him, but he'd had his back to her. By the time he'd walked around the back of the car and stepped over to the concrete seawall, Meg could only stare after him. Darn it, she wanted him back here, next to her…kissing her.

Stupid Carl. Suddenly, she remembered that he was still on the line. "Yes, I'm still here, Carl. But there's nothing to discuss. I can't forgive you. And no, I won't be home early." At least, she hoped she wouldn't be. Still keeping Joe in sight, she told Carl, "I have to go. Oh, all right, fine, I'll at least think about it. Yes, I know you aren't taking this lightly. Okay, I'll call you tomorrow."

Meg jabbed the end button, turned the phone off and stuffed it back into her purse. She had no intention of calling Carl tomorrow. But she'd said she would, hoping he'd be satisfied and wouldn't leave a hundred messages on her machine. She sighed, as she studied her not-a-date's wide shoulders, broad back, slim hips. He was put together so fine. Smitten with his aura of masculine strength and power, she crossed her arms on the lowered window's sill, rested her chin on her arms and drank in her fill of him.

Thoroughly immersed in the sight he made spotlighted by a street lamp, Meg realized something. She'd been fooling herself a moment ago when she'd thought Joe Rossi could be her fling. This man was not fling material. She'd already seen enough of him—well, surmised enough about him, at any rate—to know he was a man of depth, someone who could quickly come to matter.

Damn it. Shaking off her sensual lethargy, Meg followed Joe's gaze out across the water. Directly across from him sat upscale Harbour Island with its stylish restaurants and yachts and hotel. The lights twinkled, music danced over the water and the southern night was soft. Meg wondered what Joe thought of her city. Maybe she should ask him. That would be a good start.

But first, she found her purse, located the tiny tin of mints and popped one in her mouth. She shouldn't be hoping for that kiss, but a girl never knew. With that, she got out of the car to join him, knowing he would hear the sounds the door made as she opened and closed it. Meg crossed the small, bricked parking lot and stood next to Joe, who glanced down at her and smiled, as he might if a stranger had joined him.

"So," she said with intentionally ironic cheeriness, "Carl's a jerk."

Nodding, Joe looked out over the night-blackened water. "I'm beginning to agree with you."

"He, uh, wants to get back together."

"Sounded to me like he wants to do more than that." Looking off to his left, Joe put his hands on his hips. "It's beautiful right here."

"Yes, it is. This is one of the prettiest vantage points for seeing the bay." Oh, the man had cooled considerably toward her. With her next breath, she said, "It's not gonna happen, Joe. With Carl, I mean."

Joe turned to look at her. "It's not my business, Meg. You don't owe me any explanations."

"I know I don't. And I know I keep saying this isn't a date, but it was starting to feel like one back there in the car, wasn't it?"

"Yeah. But he asked you to marry him. A man doesn't do that lightly."

Joe's vaguely accusatory tone, so close on the heels of Carl's aggravating, mood-shattering phone call, had Meg crunching her breath mint and saying what she thought. "So, I should call him back and say yes, just because he asked? I don't think so. I broke up with him. He only asked because he doesn't like to lose. That's all. Trust me, if I'd said yes, he'd already be running for the next plane to…Bora Bora."

Joe inclined his head quizzically. "Bora Bora?"

Meg shrugged. "It's the first remote-sounding place that came to mind."

He nodded, a crooked grin breaking through briefly. "I'm sorry I said what I did just now. The truth is, I don't get an opinion, but the whole thing still…hit me wrong."

He looked so sorry—and uncomfortable. Meg relented, going with humor to smooth things over. "Well, I can't imagine why. The woman you were about to kiss gets a phone call from another man who asks her to marry him? Gosh, I just don't see how that could be awkward for you, Joe."

He chuckled. "Go figure. But that's why I got out of the car. It sounded to me like you two still had a lot to talk about. I didn't want to get in the way."

She waved that away. "You are *so* not in the way. You couldn't be less in the way even if you were in—"

"Bora Bora?"

She nodded. "Exactly."

"Well…good." Joe turned to look out over the water again.

Meg stood silently at his side, so close she could feel his body's warmth, yet miles away. Why couldn't they get back to the part where they'd been about to kiss?

"So, what did Carl do?" Joe's question broke the silence. "Why'd you break up with him, I mean?"

Meg took a deep breath and let it out slowly. "He cheated on me. We'd been together for about a year. But last week I caught the rat out on a date. A date! Worse, the woman he was with didn't even know I existed. She thought he was cheating on her with me! Can you believe it? Obviously, neither one of us was very important to him."

"How about you?" Joe turned his head and looked

at her. "I mean, how much did you care for him before he, uh, started dating?"

His question took Meg by surprise. "How much did I care? I don't know. I guess…some. I cared enough to stay with him for a year. Is that an answer?"

"Yeah. A year is a long time. So, what if he hadn't cheated on you and had asked you to marry him tonight? Would you have said yes?"

The man could come up with some probing questions. "Again, I don't know. I guess I'd have told him I needed to think about it."

Joe nodded. "You'd have to think about it—after a year of being exclusive?"

Meg was about to say yes, but her next thought caught her up short. "Oh my God, I see what you're getting at. If I had to think about my answer, then it was probably always no, right?"

"Most likely."

"Well, what do you know—I didn't love him and was wasting my time. Joe, I owe you a big, fat thank-you for that insight."

"No big deal. I'll send you my bill. Still, Carl's a fool for cheating on you."

"You're sweet to say so. Besides, it was all so unnecessary. All he had to do was tell me he didn't want me around. How hard is that?"

Joe looked suddenly uncomfortable. "Sometimes it can be really hard, if you have any kind of a conscience, and if you suspect the other person cares for you a lot more than you do for her."

Her? He was no longer talking about her and Carl, Meg realized. "So, Joe. You sound like you know how that feels."

He exhaled roughly. "I do. Meg, I think I should tell you something. There's… Well, I have a… Okay, her name's Linda."

3

"Oh." Joe's words hit Meg like a slap to the face. "I see. You have a Linda. How nice. Is she your—" Meg winced "—wife?"

"Oh, hell no, nothing like that. We've been together now for about six months…and she wants the relationship to be more."

"I see. Well." A sudden sense of loss made Meg want to sit down in a big, dejected heap and cry. "Maybe we should introduce Linda and Carl, since they both seem to have a case of the commitment bug. That is, unless you've caught it, too." She looked over at him.

When he didn't reply right away, Meg surreptitiously crossed her fingers against his answer—and held her breath.

Joe rubbed a hand through his hair. "I don't know. That's why I came to Tampa. Time away to think."

There was hope. Her mood suddenly lighter, Meg pointed at him. "So, that's why you were asking me all those questions a minute ago. You're looking for some insight yourself."

Joe had the grace to nod and look sheepish. "I am, yeah. But my situation is different."

"Is it? How so?"

"Well, no one's been cheating."

"Really?" Meg crossed her arms and shrugged. "Don't give up so easily, cowboy. The night's still young."

Joe laughed. "I like a woman who knows what she wants."

"Good." Though she now adopted an air of sophisticated confidence, inside Meg was quaking with the audacity of what she'd just said…and implied.

Joe's eyes twinkled. "You've certainly given me a lot to think about in the few short hours I've known you, Meg Kendall."

"Yeah? Thinking of doing something stupid, are you, Joe?"

"You mean like this?" He grabbed her by her arms and pulled her tight against him. Before she could react, he'd lowered his head and crushed his mouth against hers in a bruising, passionate kiss that curled Meg's toes and scattered her senses. His tongue explored her mouth…probing…pushing in and out…mimicking perfectly the thrusting act of sex.

People driving past *wa-hoo-ed* out their car windows or honked their horns.

Meg wouldn't have cared if an actual cheering crowd, complete with marching band, had gathered behind them. Her heart was beating triple time and her knees had become weak with desire. She was helpless, unable to resist.

When Joe broke the kiss and pulled back, Meg stared deep into his magnificent eyes. "Yeah. Like that. We shouldn't do that…again…Joe."

That quirky little Elvis grin of his appeared on his lips—lips Meg now knew intimately.

"No. We shouldn't." Joe lowered his head, and Meg raised her mouth to meet his again. But he pulled back at the last second, teasing, staring intently into her eyes.

Meg's blood heated. "Damn you, Joe Rossi."

She reached up, gripped him around the muscular column of his neck and pulled him firmly down to her. This time, she took the lead, allowing only the tip of her tongue to dart in and out as she tasted the sensual fullness of his lips. With an evilly sexy chuckle, Joe finally captured her mouth and again plundered its willing depth as he put his arms around her and held her to him, her breasts hard against his chest, her hips hard against his thighs.

And then, unbelievably, a cell phone rang.

"Aw, son of a bitch!" Joe could not believe they'd been interrupted—*again*—by a damn cell phone.

Meg pulled back, gasping. "Is that your pants ringing—or my ears?"

"My pants. In more ways than one." He gently released her and reached for the phone at his belt, tugging it off its clip. "I ought to throw the damn thing in the water."

Meg stepped away from him and hugged herself as if she were cold. "I hope Linda can swim."

Poised to push the talk button, Joe held off and looked into Meg's smoldering bedroom eyes. He was hungry to kiss her again…and not stop there. "It doesn't have to be…Linda."

He hated that he'd hesitated over her name. But right now, with Meg standing less than a foot from him, the last thing Joe was thinking about was his girlfriend. Hell, he was no better than Carl, was he?

The cell phone continued to ring.

Meg's gaze locked with his. "You might as well answer it, cowboy," she said, sounding practical. And angry.

"You're right," Joe said, resigned. He pushed the button and put the phone to his ear. "Hello." To his infinite relief it wasn't Linda. It was... "Uncle Maury!"

Meg looked at him questioningly. Joe shrugged. He had no idea why his great-uncle would be calling him. Then, when he heard the tone of Maury's voice, he tensed. "Wait. Slow down. What are you saying? What mob?"

"A mob?" Meg said. "At the complex? Does he mean a party at the pool?"

Joe shook his head and held up a hand to Meg. "Oh, I get it. Not a mob, but *the* mob?" His tensed muscles relaxed. "No, Uncle Maury, we're not doing this. You know there's no mob at the door."

Meg clutched Joe's shirtsleeve. "Is he okay?"

Joe covered her grasping hand with his free one and nodded, mouthing *I think so.* He turned his attention back to his great-uncle. "Well, just don't answer it," he told Maury. "What do you mean we can't come home? We weren't on our way home.... Not ever? Uncle Maury, have you been drinking?"

"What's going on?" Meg hissed.

"Hold on, Uncle Maury. Let me talk to Meg. Don't hang up." Joe released Meg's fingers and held his hand over the phone's mouthpiece. "Uncle Maury says we can't ever come home because the mob is after him— and now they're after us because we're in The Stogie," he said matter-of-factly. "He means the car," he added.

Meg shook her head, looking confused. "But Maury's called The Stogie, not the car."

"They both are. I think Uncle Maury's letting his imagination get the best of him."

Meg pulled back. "But he always talks about the mob."

"Yeah, but this is going a bit too far." Aware of his elderly uncle hanging on the line, Joe spoke quickly to Meg. "You see, there's a legend in our family that someone, at some time in the past, was in the Mafia. Uncle Maury decided he was that person and we've always gone along with it. It gave him stature. But he's never made phone calls like this saying the mob is after him or anyone else. This is new."

Concern shadowed her expression. "Maybe he didn't take his medicines. Or maybe he took too many. I knew we shouldn't have left him alone. Joe, tell him not to do anything. That we're on our way home right now."

Joe nodded and put the phone to his ear. "Uncle Maury? Meg says just sit tight, okay? We're on our way home."

Blinking, Joe jerked the phone away from his ear and said to Meg, "Whoa. He's cussing like crazy. Listen." He put the phone to her ear, saw her eyes widen, then pulled it away.

"Tell him we won't come home, if that's what he wants."

"Sure, why not. Let's go back to the car." He grasped Meg's arm to guide her and again spoke to his uncle. "Uncle Maury, listen to me— No, we're not coming home…. Yes, calm down. It's okay. No, I'm not lying. What? Shoot at us?" Joe's knees locked, stopping him and Meg in their tracks, and he shook his head in disbelief.

"Shoot at us?" Meg parroted. "Who's going to shoot at us?"

Joe held Meg's fear-widened gaze as he talked. "Now, Uncle Maury, why would anyone be shooting at us?" He paused. "They want the keys? To what, the car? Uncle Maury, if anyone wants the keys to this car, trust me, I'll hand them over long before they have to start shooting. Not the car keys? But don't give them up, either? Well, what else would I have keys to, that some— How much money?"

Joe covered the phone and whispered to Meg. "He says the keys are worth a fortune."

"Forget that. I want to know who's going to shoot at us."

"Apparently the mob."

"Okay, Joe, this is beyond bizarre. And a little scary, I have to say."

"Tell me about it. But such is life with Maury Seeger."

"Well, what do we do? Do we believe him or not?"

"I don't know. Something's wrong, I'll give him that much. Something definitely set him off."

"Yeah, and it could be nothing more than some poor pizza delivery guy at his door."

"True. And Maury could shoot him."

Meg's eyebrows rose. "Maury has a gun?"

"Yes."

"Dear God."

"Amen."

"Joe?"

"What?"

She pointed to the phone in his hand. "Talk to Maury."

"Oh, hell." He put the phone to his ear. "Hey, Uncle— What?" He listened another moment and then pulled the phone away from his ear and hit the end button. "He said he thinks they're trying to get inside and he has to go. Then the line went dead."

"Ohmigod," she breathed. "Joe, could it really be the Mafia?"

"I think Uncle Maury is harmless, but sometimes the way he gets caught up in his stories worries me—" Joe's phone rang again. He exchanged a look with Meg and answered it on the second ring. "Uncle Maury? Is that you?" He nodded at Meg to let her know it was.

She looked so concerned, waiting to find out what Maury would say next, that Joe couldn't resist putting an arm around her and pulling her close. He wasn't sorry when the action squeezed her breast against his side.

"Really, Uncle Maury, did you have to hang up a minute ago? Are you okay? Your voice sounds funny…. You're in the men's room at the pool house? Why? What are you— Of course, you're hiding. Look, stay there where you feel safe. Uncle Maury? Hello? You just dropped the phone? Why'd you drop the phone?"

He listened and then said to Meg, "Because he thought the mobsters were shooting at him, but it turned out to be a car backfiring."

Meg leaned into him. "I might need to sit down, Joe."

He took her arm to steady her and returned his attention to his great-uncle. "Is anyone else in there with you, Uncle Maury? Hell, no, I wasn't suggesting you and another man— Yes, I do know how it would look for two guys to exit a one-holer bathroom together. Look, just sit tight and—"

Joe pulled the phone away from his ear. "Son of a— The line went dead again. When we get to his place, Meg, I swear I'm going to kick his ass. I don't care if he is in his eighties and only five feet tall. I'm still going to kick his bowlegged, Mr.-T-gold-wearing, toupee-headed ass. Come on, let's go see about my great-uncle, the nutcase."

THEY WERE IN THE CAR with its front-mounted vanity plate that read "The Stogie" and on the way back to Meg's apartment complex when she first became aware that she and Joe were being followed. Or, at least, she thought they were.

"Joe? Do you see—"

"Yes."

Meg's breath caught. "Oh my God, we *are* being followed."

"I don't really think so. Try not to let my crazy uncle, with all his mobster talk, get to you, okay?"

Too late for that. Meg turned to look over her shoulder at the occupants of the car behind them. "I kept seeing their bright lights in the side-view mirror, and I wondered."

"Same here. Funny how quickly someone else's paranoia can infect your mind, isn't it? Still, maybe you shouldn't turn around and stare at them." Joe's voice was level, like the patient one a parent might use to reassure a small child convinced that his bedroom closet held a monster. "And why aren't you wearing your seat belt? Turn around and put it on, okay?" He glanced in the rearview mirror and then over at her. "No sense alerting them that we're onto them."

"Do you think we're really being followed?" she asked, more interested in the action going on behind them than in his safety instructions.

"I really don't."

"Well, it's possible." Excitement and fear had Meg melting down onto the bench seat. From this new vantage point, she looked up at Joe. "Why can't the car behind us just be a bunch of innocent people who're going the same way we are?"

Joe looked over at her—or where she should have been—and then down to where she was. A puzzled frown claimed his features. "They could be. What are you doing?"

"Clearly, I'm hiding. Besides, I got a good look at those people. What we've got are two guys *dressed in black* on our tail."

"Mobsters aren't the only people who wear black. I occasionally wear black. Maybe these guys are some partying Goths heading to a nightclub."

She stared at Joe's profile, absorbing his handsome features. "But maybe they aren't."

"There's one way to prove it to you."

Meg became aware of another sensation. "Are you slowing the car down, Joe?"

"Yes. If these guys behind us are two partying Goths on their way to a night of clubbing, then they'll be in a hurry to get around us, won't they?"

"Yes." Meg was silent, allowing for time and

events to pass. When she couldn't stand the suspense anymore, she said, "They didn't pass us, did they?"

"No."

"Oh, God." But judging by the squealing tires and all the curses being flung their way, everyone else in Tampa was in a hurry to get around them. Meg heard Joe muttering something back at the other drivers, but it was nothing she could actually make out.

"So, Meg," he said abruptly, "I have to wonder what the two guys in the really slick car behind us think you're, uh, *doing* right now, since you've disappeared from view in the front seat."

It took her a second, but she finally got his drift—and her face burned. She popped upright and fingercombed her hair out of her face. "Is this really the time to be amusing yourself with pornographic thoughts?"

He spared her a quick grin. "I was just trying to get you to sit up and put on your seat belt, which you still need to do."

Soberly, Meg said, "I think we ought to go to the police."

"Because of what I just said? Really?"

"No, because if these guys behind us are with the—and I use *this* word every day—mob, then we should find a police station. Every woman knows, or should, that if she's being followed, she heads for the nearest police station."

Joe stopped and thought for a moment, then nodded slowly. "Okay. Where's the nearest station?"

Meg thought about it and shrugged. "I have no idea." Joe leveled a look at her and then concentrated on the road. "Well, I'm sorry. I haven't been followed before. This is new to me."

He reached for her hand and squeezed it. "I'm sorry. Look, don't worry about it. Can you actually see us going to the police with this story? What would we tell them? My sweet but crazy-assed great-uncle thinks the Mafia is after him—and us—because we have keys to something that contains a lot of money? What would you do if you were the cops and someone came into the station with that story?"

"I'd bust them for being high and lock them up."

Loving his warm touch and the feel of his strong fingers clasped over hers, Meg held on to Joe's hand. For just a moment, she let herself imagine how those same hands would feel on her body. Then, focusing again on their current plight, she said, "Maybe we need to take Maury seriously for just a few minutes. I mean, I know he's the king of exaggeration, but maybe there's a grain of truth to this tale."

Joe riveted his gaze on her for far longer than it was probably safe to do while driving. "Meg, do you really think the *mob* was there and pounding on his door? I mean would they really want all the attention they'd get from about five hundred of his closest neighbors if they did that?"

She eyed him suspiciously. "You seem to know a lot about how the Mafia works, Joe."

He took his hand back and put it on the steering wheel, holding it tight. "I've probably seen the same movies you have."

Meg flushed with self-consciousness. "Touché. Still, what if something's up—"

"Meg. Pizza delivery guy at the wrong door. Car backfiring. Nutty, paranoid great-uncle, whom I love very much, put two and two together and came up with the mob. End of story. What we're going to do is go to his place and see for ourselves what's up. So, please, buckle your seat belt."

She quickly stretched the nylon straps across her chest and lap and snapped the buckle into place. "Okay. Done."

"Good. Hold on. I'm going to speed up."

Sure enough, the car jumped forward with a lurch and a stutter that wrenched Meg back and then forward and nearly made her bite her tongue. Once she regained her equilibrium, she gave voice to her current thought. "Joe, how can these guys behind us be the mob if they're at the apartment with Maury?"

Joe changed lanes, moving to the inside-left one. "You're not going to let this go, are you? All right. I suspect, Meg, that if it's the Mafia we're really dealing with, they probably have more than two members."

"Good point." She felt so dumb—and tried to cover it. "But how many of them do you think they'd send after one little old man?"

"Depends on the little old man. And what he might have of theirs."

"True. Are we still being followed?"

He glanced into the rearview mirror. "If you mean is the same car still behind us, then yes it is."

A chill washed over Meg. "Okay, that's it. Pick a street and turn onto it. Don't signal. We need to give them the slip. If they just go on by and don't try to follow, then we have our answer. But if they stick with us, then we'll know that they really are after us."

Joe shot her a quick glance. "What were you—a gun moll in a past life? Think, Meg. If they are supposed to be Mafia, and they are following us, and there are other—I do not believe I'm even saying this—*gangsters* with my uncle, then these guys behind us already know exactly where we're going. There's no point in trying to lose them."

"Darn. You're right. So what are you going to do?"

"Exactly what I said. We'll go to my uncle's."

She watched Joe for a minute, focusing on the curve of his cheek and the strength evident in his jaw. "Joe, if we don't make it out of this alive, I want you to know one thing. You're a really great kisser."

He grinned. "Thanks. So are you."

IN LESS THAN TWENTY MINUTES, Meg stood with Joe in the dining room of Maury's apartment. The Goths, or whoever the innocents had been in the car behind them, had finally turned off, to Meg's infinite relief, so they'd made it here without further incident…only to find the elderly man gone.

Before coming inside, Joe had checked the men's room of the complex's community pool, only to find it empty, too. But the note they found on Maury's dining room table in the tidy apartment—no sign of a struggle—stated where he was. "On the run from the mob."

Meg stood rigidly at Joe's side, peering around his arm at the note in his hand. "Oh, no." Her voice was breathless with fear and worry. "He was telling the truth."

Joe frowned. "He asked me to feed his goldfish."

"Well, how thoughtful. And odd." Still, she looked from Joe to the note, like she might find a clue she'd missed. "If he was able to write this note, I guess they never made it into his apartment."

"Meg, there is no 'they.' This is Uncle Maury's idea of a joke. Or, worse, a scavenger hunt."

"A scavenger hunt?" What was Joe talking about? She studied his profile. Yes, he was very handsome but he might also be very nuts. Like his great-uncle. She remembered Wendy talking about Maury and Joe being from the same murky gene pool. "No matter what's going on, your uncle's missing. Shouldn't we be worried?"

"If he doesn't show up soon, we should. But reading this note, Meg...well, it's more like it's just some big game he's devised and he wants us to chase him all around town finding clues."

Now she understood what he meant about a scavenger hunt. She let her gaze play over his chiseled features again. He was back to being unbelievably handsome, and not nuts at all.

She again studied the slip of paper. "You got all that out of his note?"

"I told you, he's done this before," Joe continued. "When I was a kid and the family would all be together, he'd make up cops-and-robbers games just like this. He'd hide from us and have us kids running all over the place looking for him because he had the prize."

"What was the prize?" Meg realized it probably wasn't the most relevant question right now, but she couldn't help herself.

Joe's blue eyes bored meaningfully into hers. "The same thing it is now. Money."

4

MEG BRACKETED HER WAIST with her hands. "Are you kidding me? Money? So, this is all a game to him? Here we're worried sick and he's getting a big laugh from it? If you're right, when we find him, *I'm* going to kick his ass, the little stinker."

"Feel free. But let me think out loud a minute and figure out where we are, all right?" When Meg nodded, he continued. "Okay, he told us not to come here. Which he knew we would. So he left us this note to guide us to the next clue."

"Maybe."

"Maybe?" Joe held the note up to her as if it were evidence.

Meg frowned. "I'm having trouble seeing the game in all this, Joe. Let's say, for the sake of argument, you stick with the scavenger hunt thing, I'll go with the Mafia, and we'll both consider a huge mental snafu. That way, we cover all the bases."

"Makes sense. How do you see it?"

"Well, maybe they—the gangsters who were actually here—don't know he left the note."

Joe rubbed his jaw as if that helped him to reason. "But the note was in plain view on the dining room table. How could they not see it?"

Meg shrugged. "Maybe they're dumb gangsters."

"Or not." Joe eyed her levelly. "And in your running-from-the-mob scenario, how is my uncle getting around? We have his car."

"A cab, maybe?"

Joe nodded. "That's what I'm thinking. Or maybe some of his cronies are in on this, too, and driving him around. Remember those guys he said were coming over for cards?"

"Oh, that's right. Maybe it wasn't for cards... at...all." An unexpected yawn got away from her, claiming the last few words. Embarrassed, Meg clamped her hands over her mouth. "I'm sorry."

Joe's face softened into a sweet expression of sympathy, making her heart melt.

"Hey, I'm sorry, I wasn't thinking. Look, it's after eleven already. Why don't I walk you to your door and go chase Uncle Maury down by myself? There's no reason for both of us to miss out on sleep."

Meg waved her hands in protest. "No way. I'm not missing out on the best adventure I've had in years."

"You're a good sport, but I'm not so sure of my theory that I can just toss yours out. We could be riding right into something dangerous. I don't think I could forgive myself if anything happened to you."

"I don't think I could forgive you, either," Meg assured him mock-seriously. "So don't let anything happen to me. Besides, if I'm right, I need to go with you for backup."

He sized her up and apparently found her wanting. "Backup? You?"

"Hey, don't get all macho on me. I have pepper

spray, remember, that could come in handy," Meg warned.

"Yeah, that ought to scare the hell out of a bunch of gangsters."

"Along with that little knife you don't even know how to use?"

Joe narrowed his eyes. "We're not getting anywhere trading insults."

"You started it."

"Meg."

"All right, all right." She pointed to the note in Joe's hand. "So, what do we do next?" Meg looked up at him, noticing anew the deep blueness of his eyes.

"We should forget all this and just go to bed. Let him wonder where the hell we are, instead of the other way around."

She'd stopped listening when he'd said *they* should just go to bed. Blinking away the sexy images that served up, she smiled. "But what we're really going to do is…"

Slumping tiredly, Joe scrubbed his hands over his face and then stretched mightily, presenting her with an eye-popping vision of male muscular vitality. "I'll drive, you navigate."

"I'm in."

He looked at her questioningly. "Okay, but feel free to call it quits anytime you want. I have no idea how long he'll drag this out."

"*If* it's him dragging it out."

"Okay, *if* it's him."

Though she remained skeptical, the danger just didn't seem real. Instead, a thrill of pleasure at the thought of being with Joe even longer raced over Meg's skin and revived her. "Okay. Let's get started. A minute ago you said Maury left us a clue. What is it?"

"I'm not sure. See what you make of this. He says we're to go to Mario's. Who the hell is Mario? Have you ever heard him talk about this guy?"

Meg frowned. "No. Even if he had, how are we supposed to know where some guy named— Oh, wait! Of course. I love *Mario's.*" Meg grinned. "It's not a who, Joe, it's a place. Come on. I know exactly where your uncle is."

"Then let's go."

"Not until we feed the goldfish."

FORTUNATELY, IN JOE'S VIEW, Meg had realized that Uncle Maury meant the upscale, happening restaurant and bar on busy Dale Mabry Highway. This was one big, bustling place of low lights and formally attired waitstaff. A place where liquor and laughter flowed. Where movie stars, rock stars and sports figures had signed their pictures "To Mario, with Love" or "with thanks." They didn't say for what, and Joe didn't want to know. As he watched Meg scan the room, her pretty face glowing with the thrill of the chase, her shapely hips swiveling as she carved a path through the room, he couldn't help but wish for more intimate surroundings—say, dim lights and a soft mattress.

Back in the café and bar section of the restaurant, where Joe and Meg had been seated, even more framed eight-by-ten glossies hung above intimate booths filled with classy women and tough-looking guys. He just sure as hell hoped he didn't have to exchange words with any of them. But there was no telling with Uncle Maury. In fact, Joe was beginning to fear his great-uncle did, indeed, belong with this crowd of heavies.

Unsettling him further were Meg's excited tales that actual Mafia figures were reputed to hang out at Mario's. She'd told him that the newspapers periodically reported mysterious goings-on in some discreet back room here. As she'd talked, her brown eyes had shone bright with excitement. Joe had merely grinned at this, remembering that this was the same woman who, earlier, had ducked down in the car seat at the first hint of "bad guys."

Right now, though, the place was filled with happy Friday-night revelers all jostling for position, all trying to see or be seen. Joe leaned his elbow on the wood bar and kept Meg close to his side with his other arm wound tightly around her trim waist. She didn't protest the liberty, in fact, she had just as close a hold on him. He marveled at the way their bodies seemed to fit perfectly together, and couldn't help but imagine how that would translate in bed. Joe didn't quite know yet what this meant for him and Linda, but he didn't want to go there right now. He just wanted to hold Meg and enjoy how totally right and incredibly exciting it felt. He'd deal with the whole Linda issue later, when he had a minute to think about anything aside from where the hell his great-uncle was. They'd given their drink order to one of three busy bartenders—an Italian looker named Dina, according to her name tag—and waited now while she mixed them up.

Leaning in close to Meg, his mouth almost against her ear—to anyone looking at them, he would appear to be lightly kissing her hair—Joe said, "I'm thinking Waldo would be easier to spot in here than one bow-legged little mobster or trickster, whichever he is. You don't see him, do you?"

She shook her head and turned to him, putting her lips to his ear. The intimacy of her gesture…her warm breath and sweet-smelling nearness…made Joe's knees weak. And it came dangerously close to standing another part of him up at attention. "He might not be here, but maybe another note is."

Joe pulled back to stare down at her. "Great. How the hell are we supposed to find that? I expected to see him seated in a big booth with a cigar in one hand, a drink in the other, with a handful of his waving, laughing cronies all around him. Like the joke was on us."

Meg grinned. "That would have been funny."

Joe quirked his lips. "If you say so. But he's obviously not here. So, Meg, if you were Uncle Maury, where would you be?"

She leaned in close to him again. "In jail or the White House."

Chuckling at her quick wit, so much a part of her attraction for him, Joe had all he could do not to grab her and kiss the hell out of her. But knowing this was not the time or the place, he took a deep breath and exhaled for calm and control. "Maybe we should ask the staff if he left a note or a message for us. That seems like the kind of thing he would do."

Before Meg could say anything, a loud, happy and very drunk blonde in a really skimpy skirt bumped her from behind and knocked her into Joe.

"Whoa!" Joe cried out, helping the sloppily apologetic woman away and holding on tight to Meg at the same time. "You okay, Meg?"

"Yes. But that's three times with her. The next time, I'm going to start shoving back."

Joe grinned. "Now, there's a highlight to the evening. A chick fight in a bar." He pulled money out of his front pants pocket, thinking he'd be ready when the drinks came, and froze, staring at the wad of loose bills in his hand—the ones his uncle had forced on him earlier. "What the hell?" he muttered, confused.

Meg turned to him. "What? What is it? Do you see Maury?"

"No, but look at this, Meg." Holding the money down between the two of them, Joe discreetly displayed the bills. "Remember the money my uncle gave me? I thought they were dollar bills. They're not—they're hundred-dollar bills. I had no idea until this second."

Meg gaped at the money in his hands. "That's right—you used a credit card to pay for dinner. My God, Joe, how many of those did he give you?"

He sorted and counted them. "Damn. Ten. I wonder if he even knows he gave me hundreds instead of ones." He shook his head. "That crazy Maury Seeger."

Just then, Dina, the Italian bartender, leaned toward them over the bar and placed their drinks in front of them. "Hey, did you say Maury Seeger?"

Joe quickly folded the hundreds and stuck them back in his pocket. From his other pocket, he pulled out a more appropriate denomination, paid Dina and told her to keep the change, which was twice what the drinks cost. She smiled widely and thanked him for his generosity.

Joe picked up his drink, handed Meg hers, and said to Dina, while trying not to sound like Joe Friday from the old *Dragnet* series, "Yeah, we're looking for Maury. You know him?"

Dina braced her hands on the lip of the bar and eyed him and Meg. "Sure. He comes in all the time. He's a sweetheart. Who's asking?"

Joe took a sip of his drink, then spoke. "I'm Joe Rossi—"

"And I'm with him," Meg said sharply.

Joe saw the territorial expression on her face as she stared at Dina over the rim of her glass, which she'd raised to her lips. Fighting a grin, he focused again on the petite bartender dressed in a white ruffled tuxedo shirt and black vest. "Maury's my great-uncle. He left us a note saying to meet him here." Joe took a healthy swig of his beverage and winced as the strong liquor went down. "Have you seen him tonight?"

Dina assessed him, her hazel eyes flicking up and down his body. "Maybe. Where are you from?"

"Colorado. Denver."

Dina relaxed and nodded. "Okay, you check out. Yes, Maury's been here."

A jolt of triumph shot through Joe. "He has? What'd he say?"

"He told me to tell you he'd see you at the exploding chicken."

Surely he hadn't heard her correctly. Joe leaned in toward Dina, cocking his head in confusion. "I'm sorry, but with all the noise in here, I didn't catch that. He'd see me where?"

Meg pulled him back upright and answered him. "As I'm sure *Dina* would love to tell you, it's the nickname a newspaper columnist gave a piece of modernist sculpture the city installed downtown in front of a round skyscraper everyone says looks like a big beer can."

"An exploding chicken in front of a big beer can? This is some interesting city you have here."

"I know. Isn't it totally cool? Anyway, we only have to go to the corner of Kennedy and Ashley Drive. Not very far from here." She smiled at the bartender. "Right, Dina?"

Nodding, looking knowingly from Meg to Joe, she said, "Right."

"Thank you." Meg blatantly turned her back, cutting the other woman out of the conversation. "You know what, Joe?" she said breathlessly. "I'm beginning to think you're right about this being a game. Maury's got us traveling in a big circle. One more loop and we'll be right back at the apartments."

"Well, thank God. We just might see a bed tonight." *A bed?* Again, the image of him and Meg tangled together on a mattress had his body tightening. "Or…our beds, I mean. Separate beds." He was making it worse. "Forget it. Let's go." He placed his glass on the bar, Meg did the same, and Joe tapped the bar to get Dina's attention. "Hey, thanks."

She shrugged. "Think nothing of it. It's what I'm here for."

"Really?" Meg said, her voice a notch higher. "I thought it was to—"

"We're outta here." Joe gripped Meg's elbow, ready to haul her off before she vaulted right over the bar. But before he walked away, he thought of something else he needed to ask the bartender. "Dina, how'd my uncle seem? Was he okay?"

She laughed. "Sure. He was Maury. All bluster and good times."

"Really?" And here he was worried about the old guy going off his rocker when it was obviously a big joke. It really ticked Joe off. "Was anyone else with him?"

"Hard to tell. You can see what it's like in here." By now, she was mixing a drink order for some un-friendly-looking men who sat a few stools down the bar from where Joe stood with Meg.

"Yeah, I don't want to jam you up, but I thought you might have noticed if he had some old-guy friends along. Or anyone who might have stood out."

"No old-guy friends. But I did notice a couple of really big guys—dark suits, scary sort—hovering near him. Could have been anybody. But they stood out, even in here. I don't know if it means anything, but they left right after Maury did."

"Damn, you're right. It *does* look like an exploding chicken. As done by Picasso, maybe."

"I know." Grinning, Meg craned her neck back to look at the soaring example of shiny steel and bright yellow modern art that jutted many stories above her head. She and Joe had parked the black boat of a car on a side street in a metered slot and were waiting on the downtown sidewalk until Maury either showed up or they got some message from him. "Isn't it something?"

"I'm sure it's supposed to be." Joe abandoned the sculpture in favor of studying the street. "You usu-ally have this much traffic downtown late at night?"

Following his gaze, she watched the double pha-
lanx of cars zooming past on Kennedy Boulevard.
"Only if there's been a concert at the Ice Palace, or
whatever it was renamed—some corporate sponsor
or other, I forget who."

"Yeah, that's happening everywhere. At least we
have a warm evening for hanging around and waiting. We'd be freezing our butts off in Denver."

He was right about the weather—the night air,
even this close to midnight, remained balmy and
close, like a heated body wrapped around her. The
streets were lit by glass-globed streetlights and the
passing cars' headlamps. The only wind came from
vehicles in motion. "You know, I've never just stood
here like this at midnight in downtown Tampa," Meg
remarked. "I like it. More people ought to do it."

"Introduce them to Uncle Maury and maybe they
will," Joe quipped.

This near to him, Meg could feel the heat his body
generated. "No doubt. But, Joe, everything else aside,
you don't think he's slipping, do you? I mean mentally. I probably see him more than you do, but
you've been staying with him for three days. Have
you seen anything that worries you?"

"No, not until he did this."

"But even this, we don't know. I'd hate to think
we're having all this fun while he's in real danger,
from his own mental status or whoever."

Joe rubbed her arm comfortingly, which thoroughly warmed her, inside and out.

"Hey, the old coot is fine. Dina said he was all
bluster and good times, as usual. To me, that proves
he's being Maury and having fun at our expense."

"I hope so." Meg looked up at Joe. "I think Dina liked you."

Joe grinned. "And I think you didn't like Dina."

Meg felt her face heat. "I don't know what you're talking about. She seemed like a very nice girl."

Joe's knowing laugh didn't help Meg's pride any—but then again, neither did the yawn she once again couldn't stifle in time.

Joe grinned. "Am I boring you, Meg?"

She played down her social gaffe. "No. A bunch of third graders wore me out, that's all."

His expression sobered. "Oh, hell, that's right. You worked today. I forgot all about that. I should take you home. Seriously." He gripped her elbow.

His thoughtfulness warmed her. "I appreciate it, Joe, but we're already here. We have to wait for Maury. I need to see for myself that he's all right. I won't sleep until I do."

Joe's fingers drew slow, seductive circles around her elbow. "All right, we'll wait. But I wonder if Dina got the location right. There's no one out here but you and me."

Meg enjoyed his touch for a moment before commenting. "Oh, she got it right. You'll be glad to know there's only one exploding chicken sculpture in Tampa. And how can you say we're alone? Are you forgetting this fine, round building's illustrious security guard, who even now is watching us from his desk inside the lobby?"

"That's right." Joe released her arm and turned to wave at the man, who did not wave back. "And he looks thrilled that we're still hanging around."

"Definitely," Meg said, waving with him. "I

don't think he believed our story about being tourists."

"It's half true—in my case. It was obviously killing him that he couldn't come up with a reason to tell us to move along from a public sidewalk."

"Exactly. But we must look suspicious just standing here." Meg glanced all around. "Maybe we ought to do something."

"Like what?"

She met his gaze and saw his blue eyes glittering with awareness and suggestion. A sweet shiver slipped over her skin.

"Hey, you're shivering. Are you cold? Come here." Joe opened his arms and held them out to her.

Ignoring the fact that the air temperature had to be maybe eighty degrees, she said, "Actually, yes, I'm a little chilly."

Joe waggled his fingers. "Then come here."

Meg stepped into the shelter of his arms and smiled like a contented cat against the warm firmness of his chest. With his arms wrapped snugly around her, she relaxed, enjoying a sense of safety she hadn't felt since she'd left home to be on her own. Certainly she'd never felt this secure with stupid Carl the cheater.

When Joe took her chin in his strong hand and tilted her face up to his, another feeling took over— one far less relaxed. The moment his lips met hers, she wrapped her arms tightly around his neck and opened her mouth to him, inviting a deeper, more passionate kiss. Their tongues entwined in a moist, intimate mating, their breathing growing ragged as the security guard was forgotten. Meg felt herself melting deeper into Joe's embrace—the touch she'd been longing for.

A screech of brakes and a frantically honking car horn startled Meg into tensing against Joe's body. And then they heard him.

"Hey, Joey, Meggie, where the hell you been? Come 'ere! Hurry! We ain't got all night, you two lovebirds!"

5

MEG ABRUPTLY PULLED AWAY from Joe and met his stunned gaze. As one, they turned to face the street. Sure enough, there was Maury Seeger hanging halfway out the back window on the passenger side of a taxi that had pulled over to the curb. The elderly man's toupee, apparently attached somehow at the back of his head, stood straight up on top of his bald dome and flapped in the wind generated as he waved his short arms crazily.

"Hurry it up! Get a move on before they find us!"

Joe set Meg aside, muttering, "He better hope they find him before I can get over there. Look at him. He's absolutely fine. This is no mental breakdown, just a big game." Joe spared Meg a glance. "Stay here. This isn't going to be pretty."

She clutched at his shirt. "No. I'm going with you."

He studied her face, apparently assessing the possibility of being able to talk her out of her intentions. The cabbie really laid on his horn again, which brought the building's disgruntled security guard outside. To add to the cacophony, the traffic light turned green and cars, except for Maury's taxi blocking the right lane, started moving. Soon, drivers began honking their horns and swerving around the stationary cab.

Joe yelled something, but couldn't make himself heard over the noise. Looking irritated, he grabbed her hand and hauled her with him toward the curb. A part of Meg's mind registered how warm and strong his grip was and how, though harried, he considerately matched his steps to hers.

In only seconds, she and Joe reached the taxi, where he surprised her—for all his angry certainty that this evening's adventure was a wild-goose chase—by giving Maury a rough, affectionate bear hug.

"Uncle Maury," Joe yelled over the traffic, "you scared the hell out of us, dude. Are you all right?"

"For now, I am." He looked from Joe to Meg and back. "You kids okay?"

Smiling, Meg nodded.

"We're fine," Joe said. "A little tired and confused, though. What is this? Some game of cops and robbers like when I was a kid?"

"What? This ain't no game, Joey." Maury's faded blue eyes rounded with something akin to anxiety. "Where's The Stogie?"

Before Joe could answer, the cabbie started cursing in some Eastern-European language, waving his arms out of his lowered window, angrily signaling for the remaining cars to go around them. Finally, the light turned yellow, then red, and they gained a momentary respite from the noise. The man subsided with a grunt of satisfaction, as if his actions had brought them the relative quiet they needed to hear each other.

Joe, his expression that of a psychiatrist assessing a mental patient, spoke to his uncle in a mild tone. "You mean your car, Uncle Maury?"

"Hell, yeah, what else? Where is it? Were you followed?"

"I have no idea. I didn't look. Who would be following us?"

Maury rubbed his rough-featured face. "Jesus, Mary and Joseph, son, haven't you been paying attention?" He gripped Joe's hand where it rested on the opened window ledge. "Where's the car?"

Joe traded a look with Meg before answering. "It's parked on a nearby side street. Just around the corner. I'm sure it's fine. Now, what's up? And I mean the truth."

"All right, here's the thing. I don't know for certain, but I'm being followed by some wise guys sent down from Jersey by a guy I knew in the old days."

"Uh-huh."

"How they found me, after all these years, I don't know. But they want the money."

"Come on, Uncle Maury, don't do this."

Meg searched Joe's expression, seeing equal amounts of impatience and worry. It looked like his great-uncle had actually started to believe his own fabrication. "Maury," she said playing along, "if they want the money, give it to them."

"It ain't that simple, Meggie. The money's tied up in my legacy to Joey."

At Meg's side, Joe snapped to attention. "To me? What legacy? You mean that old jalopy?"

Maury nodded. "Among other things. Look, we can't stay here talking. You got to get away, too—only don't go back to the apartments." He turned to Meg. "I'm sorry, honey, that I got you mixed up in this." He focused again on Joe. "You too, kid." Then, as if he'd experienced some change of heart, his expression crumpled. "Aw, what am I thinkin' here? What am I doin', putting you kids in danger?" He held out a hand expectantly. "Give me the keys to the car. You take the cab. It's me they want. I'll take 'em on a chase while you kids get somewhere safe where you can stay until this thing is over."

Though Maury's words could have come straight from a 1930s movie script, he'd never sounded more lucid. Or more in control of his faculties. It seemed the mask of a doddering, pleasant old man had slipped away to reveal the Mafia don underneath. Was that possible? Which one was the real Maury?

"No," Joe said, holding the door shut each time Maury tried to open it. "I'm not giving you the car. You're going home right now in this cab, and we'll follow you in The Stogie."

Maury frowned furiously, then reached into the seat behind him. "If you won't take the cab, at least take your bags—"

"*Our* bags?"

Maury stopped to turn to Meg. "Yeah. I packed some things you might need—"

"You went into my apartment?" His getting Joe's stuff, she could understand since he was staying with Maury. But *her* stuff? "How'd you get inside?"

"That ain't important right now, Meggie."

"It's not?" She wasn't sure she liked this unexpected breaking-and-entering side of Maury Seeger. "Then, what is?"

"Where you're going is."

Joe took it from there. "And where do you think it is we're going?"

"I don't know, and I don't want you to tell me, but don't leave the Bay area, okay? Just find a place to stay for the night. You got the money I gave you earlier, Joey?"

Beside Joe on the sidewalk, Meg could feel the tension thrumming through his body.

"Yeah, that was quite the fistful of hundreds you pressed on me. There's no Mafia or anyone else, is there? You planned this whole thing, right down to the money I'd need during the chase."

Maury vehemently shook his head no. "You're wrong. I had no idea, I swear. This all came down after you two left earlier. I gave you that money out of the goodness of my heart and nothing else. Come on, Joey, this is me—your old Uncle Maury. I would never purposely get you or Meggie into this. How can you think that? I love you both like you're my own children."

"Oh, how sweet," Meg crooned, her heart moved by Maury's sentiment. "I love you, too, Maur—"

Honking, blaring car horns cut her off. The traffic light had turned green again.

"Son-of-a-bitchin' drivers," Maury fumed. "Look, I got to go. You get where you're going to stay for the night—"

"Forget that. I'm going to sleep in my bed at your place tonight, Uncle Maury—"

"No, you're not, Joey, you hear me? Get someplace safe and call me on my cell phone."

"Joe," Meg said softly, putting a hand on his arm, "just agree. Don't upset him."

Joe met her gaze and exhaled sharply. "All right, Uncle Maury, all right. What else?"

"Don't call the house, 'cause I got caller ID on that line. It could give you away if the wise guys get inside my place and start searching around. You two kids stay together at all times, the both of you. And remember your old Uncle Maury loves you."

"We love you, too." Joe backed away from the cab, drawing Meg with him. "Where are you going to be?" he called to his uncle.

"At my apartment!"

"Oh, that reminds me, Maury," Meg said. "We fed Larry, Moe and Curly, like you asked us to in your note."

"Good girl, Meggie." With that, Maury soundly hit the back of the front seat, turning his ire on the cabbie. "Hey, you up there, what are you—asleep? You can't hear all that honking? Let's go!"

Apparently, the driver was awake, because the taxi shot forward, nearly hitting a car that whipped into its lane ahead of it. The cab lurched to a sudden stop and just as suddenly made another shot forward that carried Maury's exuberant cursing back to Meg and Joe. Within seconds, the vehicle disappeared over a short bridge that arched over the Hillsborough River, leaving relative quiet in its wake.

Standing there on the sidewalk, Joe shook his head. "I am so sorry, Meg. Looks like Uncle Maury's up to his old tricks."

"You still think so, Joe? He acted like he knew what he was talking about."

"That's how he sucks you in. He's being consistent and his story is following a logical course. Can't fault him there." Looking troubled, Joe shook his head. "I cannot believe I had him and let him get away. I should have pulled him out of that cab and taken him with us."

"I don't think he would have let you, Joe. Besides, he said he's going home, which is where you would have taken him."

"True. Man, I don't know what the hell to tell my parents when I get home."

"About what?"

"Uncle Maury's status. My mom wants him to come live with her and Dad in Denver. She worries about him being alone and getting too old to take care of himself."

Meg smiled. "That's nice of your mom—but Denver, really? Talk about culture shock. Maury loves Florida."

"I know." Joe smiled warmly at her. "I'm beginning to see why, too."

Suddenly shy, Meg lowered her gaze to the sidewalk and stared at her painted toenails. When Joe didn't say anything further, she looked up to find him watching her.

"Meg?"

"What?"

Joe placed a steadying hand on her arm. "I just realized—and you're not going to believe this—Uncle Maury forgot to give us our bags."

JOE DIDN'T RELAX until they'd made it safely to the new chain hotel Meg had directed him to on the fringe of Ybor City. However, now that they were checked in to their clean and tidy room and had called Uncle Maury, who seemed calmer, things weren't going so well. At least, that was Joe's assessment of the current argument between him and his unhappy roommate.

Meg stood at the end of the massive, inviting king-size bed and faced Joe, her arms defiantly crossed. "I'm not sleeping in that bed with you—or in the nude either—Joe Rossi, so you can just forget that."

"Forget what? I didn't plan this." Propped against a stack of pillows, Joe was stretched out on the bed, his hands behind his head, his ankles crossed. "You're the one who said we should come here. And I did ask you to come inside with me to the check-in desk—"

"But *Mr. and Mrs. Smith?* Without luggage or wedding rings? At one in the morning? Do you know how that looks?"

"I have a pretty fair idea, since I was the one doing it. But why all the objections now, Meg? I came outside and told you, before we ever came up here, that all they had was one room with a king-size bed."

Her angry expression bled to one of hesitancy as she looked everywhere but at him. "I know. It just looks so…real now. When we were downstairs, it didn't seem that big a deal."

Acutely conscious that they were alone in a hotel room on a balmy night with palm trees swaying seductively right outside the window, Joe thought he understood. "It would have helped if Uncle Maury had at least given us our bags, wouldn't it?"

"A little." The vexation returned to her features. "And how *did* he get in my apartment, do you suppose?"

Joe shrugged. "You got me. I can't take the blame or the credit for anything he does, Meg. The man had almost sixty years to get weird before I was even born."

Abruptly, she turned away from him and started to pick at a thread on the bedspread. "Speaking of weird, what are we doing here if you don't believe him and think this is just a big game?"

"Well, for one thing, you told me not to upset him and to go along with him. For another, no matter what the truth is, it's late and we're both tired. There's no sense beating our heads against my uncle's eccentricity this late at night. And, even if he is telling the truth about the Mafia being after him, there's nothing we can do about it tonight but stay hidden. That meant someplace like this—or your place. And you wouldn't hear of that, when I suggested we—"

"I can't do that. I don't—"

"I know. You don't ask men inside on a first date— although this isn't a date, as you keep telling me. And there's also the chance that Carl the jerk, who still needs his ass kicked, could drop by and make a big scene tomorrow. You don't need that… Did I forget anything?"

Meg raised her chin a proud notch. "No. But you could have dropped me off at home—Maury would never know—and then gone somewhere by yourself."

"True. I can still do that if you want me to." Joe remained absolutely still, his gaze boring into hers.

She shook her head. "No, it's too late now. We're already here."

Joe lost a battle with a grin that tugged at the corners of his lips. "Yes, we are. But maybe I ought to tell you that I still have enough of a doubt about my old uncle's story to worry that it might be true. In that case, I didn't want to take a chance and leave you alone tonight."

Meg's eyes rounded with surprise. "Oh. I… hadn't thought about that. That's really nice of you. Thanks."

"You're welcome. But let me say something else straight out so we can get past all this and get some sleep. Just because you're going to be in the same bed with me, and that's going to make me completely wild, doesn't mean I'm going to jump you or demand sex. I'm not that kind of guy. Your reputation is safe with me, Meg."

She raised an eyebrow as she demurely crossed her legs. "I know it is because you're going to sleep in that chair, Mr. I-Have-a-Linda."

Now, why'd she have to bring up Linda? Did she really think he needed a reminder of his girlfriend's existence? "Okay, no, I'm not. The only chair in here is the hard-backed one that goes with the desk. And I don't need any reminders of Linda because I'm not the one who keeps worrying about sex. *You* are." And that was when it struck him—and had him chuckling. "Wait a minute. It's not that you don't trust me, is it? You don't trust *yourself* in that bed with me. Admit it."

Meg jumped up off the bed, her face bright red. "You could not be more wrong, you conceited—"

"Like hell! I'm right, aren't I?" Joe jackknifed to a sitting position and laughed out loud, not feeling the least bit guilty for teasing her…but more than a little guilty about having completely forgotten about Linda until Meg had mentioned her.

Meg pursed her lips angrily. "You *so* are *not* right. I do not believe your ego, Joe Rossi." She looked down at her clothes. "The only issue in question right now is what I'm going to wear to bed."

"Wear your clothes."

"And walk around tomorrow all wrinkled?" She raised an eyebrow at him. "Besides, this happens to be my favorite T-shirt and I don't want to stretch it out." She thrust out her hand. "Take off your shirt."

Joe thought her tone held a note of forced bravado. He suspected it wasn't every day that she demanded a man remove an article of clothing. Unable to resist, he grinned. "You're sending mixed signals here, Meg."

"Only in your head," she said with a roll of her eyes. "I just want to sleep in it, you big goof. Unless you mean to."

"No. You can have it." Suddenly, the image of her in his shirt…and nothing else, filled his mind. Oh, this being alone in a hotel room with her was not getting any easier. "Hey, this won't be the first time you've seen me without my shirt, will it?"

"You're not supposed to bring that up. You said it was in the vault." She put that tough-girl look on her face again and waggled her fingers at him impatiently. "Now, come on, take it off and give it to me."

"Hey, I think you're reading my lines."

Meg narrowed her eyes even further, but said nothing.

Grinning, Joe rose to his knees to undo his belt and the button at the waist of his pants. Not once looking away from her, he tugged his knit shirt out of his slacks and pulled it over his head. With air-conditioned air whooshing out of the vent and chilling his bare skin, Joe tossed his garment to her.

"Here you go."

"Thanks." She snagged it in midair, her gaze lingering on his bare chest before she turned away and rushed toward the tiny bathroom.

Joe resumed his reclined position on the bed and watched her go, admiring the sway of her shiny dark hair around her shoulders and the wiggle of her cute little behind as she hurried away. Just as she reached the bathroom door, Joe called out to her.

"Hey, Meg."

She turned around. "What?"

"We have another problem. I'm not wearing any underwear."

She stared at him, and her face turned red again. Joe waited patiently.

Finally, Meg blurted out, "Well, you're not going to wear mine, so you can forget that."

MEG HAD BEEN in the hotel room's minuscule bathroom long enough to conclude that all her high-and-mighty railing about Carl's cheating on her and how she'd never do that because she had too much integrity had just come back around to bite her on the butt. Not that she'd be cheating on anyone if she and Joe…well, if she and Joe. But he would be. He had a damn Linda. What did that mean, anyway? He'd never really said. Did he love her? Were they in a firmly committed relationship? Exclusively dating? Were they engaged? Was Linda just dreaming? Could intense and wishful thinking on Meg's part cause Linda to grow a huge wart on the end of her nose? If it could, she already had one.

Oh, stop it, Meg. You're despicable. Or maybe she was just human. Come on, this was a hotel room and they were two healthy young adults who were vastly attracted to each other. So what the heck else was supposed to happen here, if not sex?

Yeah. Thus bolstered, Meg started for the closed bathroom door, made it all the way over to it this time, but suddenly did a U-turn back to the tub, where she again confronted the solid barrier that was the closed door. Opening it was an act she'd already put off for as long as she could while stripping out of her clothes, folding them neatly, putting on Joe's shirt, trying not to breathe in the man's irresistibly masculine scent— a losing proposition—washing her face, running her fingers through her hair and fussing about not having her brush in here with her.

Then she'd rinsed her mouth with the hotel's complimentary mouthwash. She had also found soap and shampoo. And a shower cap. And a tiny shoe sponge. She hadn't used any of those items, but she had passed some minutes going through the minuscule basket of amenities next to the pygmy coffeemaker. Cowardly stall tactics.

Blame her lusting thoughts of Joe. Sure, she'd been flirty and forward when she hadn't any clue she'd ever see him again, or that she'd be thrust into a situation that encouraged acting on her desires. But now, being in an actual hotel room with him was a whole other thing. It was like the sex was expected because the situation and the setting demanded it.

That totally wasn't romantic. And then there were her rules. No sex on the first date—sometimes not until the fifth or sixth date, and sometimes never. She just wasn't casual. She gave her heart easily, but not her body. And just in time to test that theory along came this guy, Joe Rossi, who made her libido scream, *Screw the rules! We want the man!*

Well, too bad. Joe had said he wasn't going to do anything and her reputation was safe. *How freakin' noble of him.* Why couldn't he make the first move like guys were supposed to do and take this decision out of her hands? What was wrong with him? Okay, not a damn thing. He was everything she wanted—and that put her in a tough spot, didn't it? Her choices were to step outside this room and see what happened from there— or curl up on the bathroom counter and sleep in here.

She eyed the hard, short countertop. *I don't think so.* So, with her folded clothes over her arm and her heart in her throat, Meg marched to the bathroom door and opened it. The first thing she saw, straight ahead, was a closet, which stopped her in her tracks. Because Joe's slacks hung on a hanger. His shoes, with his socks stuffed in them, were on the floor under his pants. Well, the man was no slob, she'd give him that. He was, however, now nude.

Oh, God. Meg squeezed her eyes closed and held her breath for a calming ten seconds. When she exhaled and opened her eyes, she realized something else: The room's lights were dimmed. Oh, the man was very subtly sending out a signal, despite his "your reputation's safe with me" speech. He was waiting for her. Most likely she'd find him sitting up in bed, propped against pillows, only the sheet covering him from the waist down. And the look in his eyes would say, *Here I am, if you want me.*

She wanted him, damn it. It was that simple. Surely, Meg reasoned, if she and Joe felt this strongly, this quickly, he'd break it off with Linda as soon as possible. Of course, Carl hadn't with her. Not that Joe was Carl. He wasn't, but—

Ohmigod—Carl! Meg's breath caught in her throat. *He asked me to marry him. I'm supposed to talk to him tomorrow. What must Joe be thinking about that? To him, I probably seem more committed to someone else than he is.*

All right, that settled it. This situation was just too complicated and—decision made—there wasn't going to be any sex. There. That was easy, especially since she'd known the man only a matter of hours, even though it felt like three lifetimes already. But none of that mattered. She'd tell him they both needed to be free of entanglements, no matter how tenuous, before they explored this whatever it was between them.

But as she thought of the smoldering man in her bed waiting for her, Meg wondered if she could maybe rush along the tying up of loose ends—right now, tonight—by working in a quick call to Carl to tell him to drop dead. And then she could get Joe to do the same thing with Linda. Because she had a feeling that her rules were about to snap like dried twigs.

"Okay, here we go" was Meg's whispered encouragement to herself.

Her cheeks aflame with desire, her heart pounding, she resolutely rounded the corner and entered the bedroom area. Certain she could feel those hot, hot eyes of his boring into her person, making her feel naked, which she very nearly was, Meg's actions became stiff, belying her attempt at nonchalance as she padded over to the desk chair, laid her small pile of folded clothes on top of it and put her sandals under the chair.

All her tasks were now done. There was nothing left to do but go to bed. Go to Joe Rossi in her bed.

Meg straightened up, subtly squaring her shoulders. She was going to do this, and damn the consequences. She'd wanted this man from the first moment she'd seen him in that fitting room two evenings ago. Everything inside her just exploded when she was around him. She'd never had such a strong reaction to a man.

She deserved some good, clean fun. Meg shook her head the tiniest bit. No, good clean fun was a ride on a Ferris wheel. This was…a ride on a bucking stallion, with any luck. *Oh God, Meg, do it now!* She zipped around, prepared to throw her head back and offer herself up on the altar of—

What the—? Joe was sound asleep. Covered to his chest with the sheet, lying on his back, his arms and legs flung out like a starfish, he was also taking up most of the bed. And snoring softly.

An insane giggle bubbled up in Meg's throat. She felt like a silly fool. Here she'd thought she was Miss Irresistible, and all Joe wanted to do was sleep. When the barely contained hysterics subsided, she padded over to the bed, lifted the covers only enough to allow herself to slip in, and turned her back to Joe. Oh, well, she consoled herself, at least she hadn't broken any of her rules.

Before turning out the light—he'd considerately left on the one on her nightstand—Meg lay there a moment, thinking…and decided she had to know. Ever so slowly, she turned onto her back, carefully lifted the sheet…and looked. Her eyes widened. Damn Joe Rossi for a liar! He *was* wearing underwear—blue-plaid boxers, to be exact.

Irrationally angry, feeling betrayed and denied,

Meg dropped the sheet and flounced over onto her side, facing away from him again. She turned off the light, punched her pillow, then settled into the bedding—and thought she heard a low chuckle coming from the other pillow.

6

ONE SECOND Meg was sound asleep in her bed, and the next she was sitting up, wide awake, listening to someone pound fiercely on her bedroom door. Blinking rapidly, she forced her eyes to focus in the dim, opaque grayness of the room. Were those blackout curtains covering the windows? She hadn't put up blackout curtains. Thoroughly confused, she surveyed the room. This wasn't her bedroom. And she wasn't alone in the bed. Cautiously, she looked closer at the handsome, half-naked man on her left who was now also sitting up looking confused.

Oh, thank God—Joe. Last night's events came flooding back into Meg's consciousness...along with the memory that she'd spent the night lying spooned against him, but not in the usual way. He hadn't exactly wrapped himself around her. Instead, she'd thrown her arm and leg over *him.* And, she vaguely recalled, it had felt way too good to be just an innocent seeking of warmth.... Oh God, she hoped he didn't have any waking recollection of that—

"What the hell?" Joe muttered, not glancing her way, his morning-husky voice sending delicious shivers up her spine. He scratched his head and yawned.

Meg grabbed his bare arm—

Startled, Joe jumped, thrashing the bedcovers.

"Joe, it's me—Meg. There's someone at the door," she whispered.

Slumping, Joe stared down at her, obviously still not alert enough to comprehend the full scope of the situation. "Meg? What are you—? Did we—?" He glanced down at the shirt she still wore, his eyes turning a dark, dangerous blue when her traitorous nipples hardened at his gaze.

She crossed her arms self-consciously. "No, we didn't. Now, focus, Joe. Please. There's someone at the door."

"Who?"

"How would I know—" Another round of insistent pounding made Meg clutch his arm again. "Joe, I think it's the mob."

Joe covered her fingers with his warm, strong hand and sighed. "Stay here. I'll go see—"

"No, I'm going with you."

Joe stared at her like she was nuts. "It's maybe ten steps, Meg. I think you'll be fine."

"I know I will, because I'm going with you."

Before their back-and-forth could escalate, a rough male voice out in the hallway called out "Room Service!"

Joe grinned. "See? It's just Room Service. What'd you order? I'm starved." He started to get out of the bed—

And Meg pulled him back. "Joe. I didn't order anything."

Confusion marked his features. "Then why—"

"I don't know why. Worse, there *is* no room service here. Only a self-serve, free-for-all continental breakfast thing where you have to fight for food you'd never order, if you had a choice, and then eat in the lobby with people you've never met before. I hate that. It's gross."

"I'll try to remember that." Joe's sober expression emphasized the sexy-as-hell stubble covering his jaw and chin. "But on another note…" He called out to the door, "Hey, we didn't order anything. You've got the wrong room."

"No, I don't. What I got out here has your name on it."

"Yeah? What's my name?"

That silenced the man in the hallway.

Very quietly and calmly, Meg said, "It's them, and we're going to die."

Joe raised his eyebrows. "Are you always this up-beat in the morning?"

"Only when the Mafia's at the door before coffee. What are we going to do?"

"I don't know about you, but I'm going to put on my pants and go have a chat with Mr. Annoying out there."

Meg peered around Joe to the door, searching its wood grain as if it might contain clues to what was on the other side. "He's awfully quiet right now. What do you think he's doing?"

"Probably loading his gun."

"Do you really think so?"

Joe just tugged her to him.

"I'm just kidding. The guy's probably from a take-out place and has realized he got the wrong room number and left. I'm sure it's something simple like that."

Unconvinced, Meg pulled away from the solid warmth of Joe's body. "Really? How about if he just wants us to think he's gone and he's really still right outside the door and waiting for you to open it to check?"

Joe shrugged. "You could be right. Why don't *you* put on your pants and go see what's happening out in the hallway?"

Meg smacked his arm. "Because I'm not the guy here, lazybones."

In that same second, someone out in the hall knocked on the door, this time more civilly.

"That's it," Joe said. "I've had it. I haven't even had coffee yet. Wait here, Meg—and don't argue with me, for once."

With that, he rolled out of the bed and, clad only in his boxers, went to the door and called out, "Who the hell are you and what do you want? If I don't like your answer, I'm calling the cops—you got me?"

While Joe was doing all that, Meg had also rolled off the bed on her side. She'd padded quickly to her purse, where she dug out her pepper spray. By the time Joe finished speaking, she was standing right behind him, her defensive weapon at the ready. Giving her a brief glance of exasperation, he put a protective hand out to keep her firmly behind him.

Just then, a different voice from the other side of the door said, "You don't need to call the cops. I'm already here. Open up. It's about Maury Seeger."

"Oh my God," Meg breathed. "Something's wrong with Maury."

"Like hell it is," Joe whispered. "A second ago, this guy—or another guy with him—said he was Room

Service." Joe peeked out through the peephole. "I can't see anyone. Either they're really short, or they're standing to one side."

Meg had never felt so bleak inside. "We're in big trouble here, aren't we?"

"I think so. Uncle Maury might have been telling the truth."

"Oh, God. Just see what they want, Joe, and give it to them."

"And then what? They just say thanks and walk away? I doubt it. We need to keep our leverage with them."

"Our leverage? What would that be, again?"

"Beats the hell out of me. The car, maybe? Anyway, what we need is a plan to get them to go away somehow, so we can, too."

"Okay, here's a thought. You could call the real cops, like you told them you would."

"Yes, I could. And say what, exactly? 'Help, the Mafia has us stuck in our hotel room and is trying to deliver breakfast!' How do you see that going over down at the precinct? Don't you think they'd have more questions for us than they would them?" He jerked his head toward the door to indicate the guys outside the room.

Again the men outside knocked on the door. "Open up. I'm telling you, I'm a federal agent. You want to see my badge?"

Out the side of his mouth, Joe whispered, "Like those can't be faked." Then, loudly, he said, "Look, buddy, you're not a federal agent. A minute ago your pal said he was from Room Service."

"What pal? There's no one out here but me."

"I have pepper spray," warned Meg bravely and loudly, ignoring Joe's raised eyebrows and his muttered, "What the hell are you doing?"

"Good for you," their visitor replied. "You might need it at some point. But I should warn you I'm an armed officer and use of my weapon could become necessary should you attempt to assault me."

Meg's breath caught in her throat. "He'd kill us," she whispered. "Do something."

"I say we get dressed and get out of here."

To the tune of another round of knocking on the door and calls to open up, Meg hurried toward the little pile of clothes she'd left on the room's desk chair.

"Meg?"

She turned around to the sight of Joe standing half-naked before her—wide shoulders, sculpted pecs, and six-pack abs. She didn't respond, just stared.

"My shirt." He pointed at her. "You have it on. I need my shirt."

"Right." As requested, she pulled his shirt over her head and tossed it to him. Quickly, she lifted her T-shirt from the chair, grabbed up her bra from under it and slipped her arms into it. "How are we going to sneak out of here, Joe? We can't go out that door."

Standing close behind her, he didn't say anything, but now it was his turn to stare. She looked down at herself…unclasped bra, bikini panties… And a moment ago she'd just flashed him her breasts. She snapped her fingers in his face. "Focus, sweetie. This is life or death."

Dressed only in his knit shirt and boxers, Joe gave

his head a tiny shake. "Right. We'll go out the bathroom window, if it's big enough."

She shook her head. "It's not."

"How do you know?"

"Because there isn't one. But even if there was, what floor is this, again?"

"Damn it. The fourth."

A cell phone suddenly rang, making them both jump.

"Oh my God, if that's Carl—"

"I'll kill him myself. Maybe it's Uncle Maury."

"That's more likely, since the ringing is coming from over there." Meg pointed to the nightstand on Joe's side of the bed.

"Gotcha." He dove across the bed, grabbed up his phone and rolled over onto his back to face her. "You keep getting dressed."

"Don't worry. That was totally my plan." Meg managed to get her bra snapped and her T-shirt tugged over her head.

"Hello," Joe said abruptly into his phone. "Listen, Uncle Maury, there are a couple of goons with pieces— Linda!"

JOE MET MEG'S GAZE across the room. She stood there, frozen, with her khaki pants in her hands, ready to shrug into them. Barely able to look away from her tanned and shapely legs, he signaled, with a shake of his head, that he couldn't believe the timing. Turning away from Meg, he realized Linda had asked him a question.

"Uh, nothing, no. Just woke up… I sound funny?"

The guy out in the hall banged on the door. "Open up in there. This is the last time I'm going to tell you."

Joe's abdominal muscles tensed. "No, it's the TV. Some old gangster movie is on— I don't know. Are you all right?"

Yes, he knew he needed to get her off the phone, but he was momentarily too rattled to think how to do that without arousing Linda's suspicions. He didn't want her to call him back—or worse, call Uncle Maury, who might tell her what was going on. Especially the part about Joe's being in a hotel room with another woman.

Speaking of the other woman...

While murmuring polite noises as Linda talked about work and her mother's yappy little dog's skin condition, Joe stood up and looked for Meg. She was over by the bathroom and tugging his slacks off the hanger. Completely dressed now herself, she hurried toward him, but Joe shot forward, crossing the room first and turning her around. Brooking no mutiny, he urged her ahead of him into the bathroom.

Once in there, he closed and locked the door. At least in here, they were out of the line of fire...he hoped. And he didn't want Meg thinking he'd gone off into the bathroom alone to have a private conversation with Linda. He looked over at Meg, and she surprised him by holding his pants open and down low so he could step into them.

Joe's admiration for her shot up. Could she be more cool-headed or practical under pressure? And frankly, her position in front of him with her face bent toward his crotch threatened to have his desire for her skyrocketing just as quickly. With his free hand on her slender shoulder, he obediently stepped into his pants, one leg at a time, fighting his body's eager reaction to her. Meg pulled up, then buttoned and zipped his pants. Done with her part, she crossed her arms and leaned against the locked door, shooting pointed get-off-the-phone-with-your-girlfriend-right-now daggers his way.

Good idea for more than one reason.

"Hey, Linda, honey, I'm sorry to interrupt, but I have to go…. Yeah, I'm glad to hear Harry's not losing his hair anymore. I know, a bald Pomeranian named Harry is not a pretty sight. But, look, babe, someone's at the door." Which was no lie, after all. "No, I'm fine. Nothing's wrong— What? No, not a good idea. Seriously. Don't fly down here to see me."

Meg rolled her eyes and turned her gaze away from his.

Damn it. "Because there's no need. Look, I'll be home in a week, and we'll talk then. That's the deal, remember? And I really do have to go. What? Oh. Yeah. Me, too. Of course I do you, too. You know that. No, I can't say it. I just can't. Not right now—"

"Oh, for God's sake, Joe, tell the woman you love her and get off the freakin' phone. We have armed barbarians at the gate, remember?"

Joe straightened his mouth into a thin line. "No one's here with me," he said into the phone while maintaining eye contact with Meg. "That was the TV…. I told you—I'm at my uncle's…. What? Well, I didn't answer his phone just now when you called there—I mean *here*—because I was, uh, in the bathroom—"

That was when Linda called him a liar and hung up on him. Joe exhaled slowly and lowered the cell phone from his ear. "That was Linda," he said need-lessly as he hit the end button and plopped the phone into his pants pocket. "I don't think we have to worry about her calling back."

"I'll say," Meg commented levelly. "So, what do we do now?"

Oh, this room was getting smaller and smaller. But in a sudden burst of inspiration, or perhaps des-peration, Joe said, "We'll call the front desk and tell them to send up Security. I don't think whoever is out there will want all that attention coming their way, so they just might leave."

"And hang around outside instead, waiting for us to come out."

"You got a better idea?"

She shook her head. "No. Call the front desk."

He retrieved his phone from his pocket, opened it…and stared at it. He met Meg's waiting gaze. "Any idea what the number is to this place?"

Meg covered her face with her hands and spoke through the web of her overlapping fingers. "We're going to die right here in this bathroom, I just know we are."

"Meg." Joe clutched her arm to get her attention. "No one's going to die, except Uncle Maury when I get hold of him— Oh, my God." A sudden thought froze Joe in place and had him staring blankly straight ahead.

Meg put a hand on his chest. "What? What is it, Joe?"

He swallowed hard. "Linda—"

"Oh, Linda again—" Meg snatched her hand away.

"No, listen. She said she'd just called me at Uncle

Maury's house and no one answered. That's why she called my cell phone."

Apparent understanding of the implications widened Meg's brown eyes. "Oh, not good. They tortured Maury and that's how they know where we are—"

"No, they didn't. Well, they might have. No, they didn't. Even if they did, it wouldn't do them any good. We didn't tell Uncle Maury where we are, remember?"

Meg frowned. "That's right. Then how'd they find us?"

Joe thought about it for a moment. "Maybe they followed us last night, and we didn't realize it."

"And waited all night before they came up?"

"Okay, so maybe they just found us this morning. The damned Stogie is right out there in the parking lot. All they had to do was drive by and see it. Sure, the odds of it happening that way are pretty slim, but then again, here they are."

"Do you hear yourself, Joe? You're talking like you believe Maury's Mafia story is real."

"I don't know what I believe, Meg. But whoever is outside that door in the hallway with those fishy stories certainly exists. And that's what we have to go with right now."

"No kidding." Meg was chewing on a thumbnail. "But what do they want with us? Why don't they just take the car?"

"They can't. I have the keys."

"Then give them the stupid keys, Joe. Open the door and toss them out."

"Really? And then they burst in while shooting? I don't think so. And not until I know where Uncle

Maury is and that he's not hurt. For now, the keys stay with me."

She patted his chest. "You're right. Never mind. But we still don't know how they found us here. And how'd they know what room we're in? The front desk wouldn't tell them that."

"Damn, that's right. They're good at this, aren't they?"

Before Meg could respond, someone knocked on the bathroom door. She jumped straight into Joe's arms.

Joe held her tight and thought furiously of possible defensive measures he could take. Fling a tiny bar of soap at them? Lasso them with toilet paper? Squirt a sample of shampoo in their eyes—

"Joey? Meggie? You two kids in there?"

Joe stilled, not comprehending at first what he'd just heard. Finally, his brain made sense of what his ears were telling it. Yes, his crazy great-uncle was standing on the other side of the bathroom door.

Meg loosened her death grip on Joe and turned her face up to his. "Did I just hear Maury talking?"

"Yes, you did."

She shook her head, looking amazed. "Could it be, Joe, that this is a nightmare and we're not really awake?"

"If there's a God." Joe set her aside, feeling as murderous as he was confused. "If you'll excuse me, Meg, I'm going to go kill my uncle."

"You keep saying that, but you never do it."

And she sounded downright petulant about that, too. "This time, I mean it. Trust me."

All it took were two determined strides across the tile floor to reach the door, unlock it and whip it open.

Sure enough, there stood short, paunchy, bowlegged Maury Seeger with his toupee askew and an unlit cigar in his hand. No big ugly ham-fisted guys flanked him. He was alone and Joe had never been so glad to see him. He proved it by saying, evenly, "I'm going to kill you now, Uncle Maury. I promised Meg I would."

"What for? What'd I do?"

Meg stepped around Joe, twitching a pointing finger in his great-uncle's face. "You." Each waggle of her finger missed hitting the tip of the octogenarian's nose by about a hairsbreadth. "What do you mean 'what'd you do?' You and your *friends* had us thinking there were Mafia hit men right outside our door. Well, I hope you all got a big laugh out of scaring us just now—and last night, too. I don't know what you're up to, Maury Seeger, or what kind of game you're playing here, but it's not funny anymore, I can tell you that. And here I thought you were my friend. I've even been defending you when Joe thought you were senile. It never occurred to me that you're just mean."

Maury's expression had become more and more grim as Meg's tirade had gone on. With a somewhat blank stare, he looked from her to Joe. "There were wise guys right outside your door? Just now?"

"Don't start, Uncle Maury. I'm warning you. Meg has pepper spray she's just itching to use. Either you come clean about how you knew we were here and about what's really going on, or I'm going to turn her loose with it."

Maury put a thick-fingered hand to his forehead. "I think I need to sit down. I don't feel so well."

Instant worry for the old man supplanted anger in Joe's heart—Meg's, too, apparently, as she rushed to take Maury's one arm while Joe supported him on the other side. Only by turning sideways in the door-frame could they all three escape the bathroom and make it into the bedroom. As one, the three of them sat at the foot of the bed with its rumpled sheets.

"You want some water?" Meg asked. "I'll get you some." She jumped up, but instead of tearing for the bathroom, she turned on Joe. "How could you let me go on like that? Now I've killed him, and I'll have to live with that—"

"Hold on," Maury interrupted, clutching her arm and tugging her back onto the bed. "I ain't dead yet. And I don't want no water, honey. I'm all right. For now, just listen to me, okay? This ain't no game I'm playing with you. Those two goons you say were here ain't friends of mine. Like I told you last night, I think someone from my past up in Jersey sent them down."

Joe could contain himself no longer. "Then where are they now? Why would they just leave? They're the ones with the guns, not us."

"I don't know where they are—"

"Wait a minute. How'd *you* know where we are? I didn't tell you when I called last night."

"Oh, that." Maury waved a hand like it was no big deal. "I had that idiot cabbie follow you here, just to make sure you made it. So sue me for caring."

"And the room number? How'd you know that?"

"Twenty dollars to the kid at the desk."

"Of course. And how'd you actually get inside the room?"

"Another twenty buys a pass key. That's why you

should always use that little latch on the chain, for extra protection."

"I'll remember that." Joe looked at Meg, who met his gaze. "This explains a lot, doesn't it? Like why we were supposed to call his cell phone and not the house. He wouldn't be there, since he was following us. It also explains how the 'hit men' out in the hall—no doubt a couple of his cronies—also knew the room number." He jerked his thumb in his great-uncle's direction. "Because this wise guy right here told them. They're all in on it, he and his friends. All it took to pull it off was a simple act of bribery."

"You got it all wrong, Joey, I swear you do."

"And you," Joe warned his great-uncle, "aren't out of hot water yet. I sure as hell haven't seen any goons or heavies or whatever the hell you call them. All I know is a couple of goofs were knocking on the door, saying they were Room Service. Then they were federal agents, and then they were gone, just like that. So, none of this is funny to me. It's way too early in the day—"

"No, it ain't. It's nearly ten o'clock in the morning."

Joe exchanged a look with Meg. "We must have been more tired than I realized."

"It's the heavy curtains," she said. "So you can sleep."

"Apparently they work." Again he settled his attention on his uncle. "The point is I wouldn't care if it was noon. I haven't yet had coffee, a decent shower or breakfast, and I'm still wearing the same clothes I had on yesterday—"

"That's why I'm here this morning."

But Joe was on a roll. "And since you weren't

home this morning—apparently, you were on your way here—when Linda phoned, she called me on my cell phone."

Maury made a face of distaste. "Oh, that couldn't have been fun. But look here—I brought your bags, yours and Meggie's. I forgot to give them to you last night. They're right over there by the door." Maury started to get up off the bed.

Joe held him in place. "Uh-uh. Not yet. Not until you give us the truth."

"But you know the truth, and we ain't got all day, Joey. We need to get out of here before those goons come back. They could be anywhere—"

"Right. Like in a coffee shop down the road, waiting to have a good laugh with you at our expense. Come on, out with it, Uncle Maury. The truth. Or we're not going anywhere."

7

THE TRUTH WAS, Meg reflected late that afternoon, they hadn't been able to get anything more out of Maury than they already knew. The man was sticking to his story that this was not a joke. It was the Mafia.

Not that she was feeling any pain about it at the moment. How stressed could someone be when sitting on warm, sunny St. Pete beach while sipping a cool drink, with a great-looking guy right in the next wooden deck-chair? A big hotel-owned, canvas sun-umbrella, its spiked end driven deep into the sand, shaded them both. No point in trying to sunbathe when they were dressed in shorts. The one thing Maury hadn't thought to pack was swimsuits. Too bad, because she would have liked to see Joe in nothing but swimming trunks, his powerful chest on display for her viewing pleasure.

"So, *Mr. Smith*," Meg said, turning slightly in her chair to see him, "at least we had a couple of pieces of luggage this time when we checked in. Tell me, what do you think of the great big pink historical hotel behind us? Pretty darn cool, huh?"

"I'll say, *Mrs. Smith*. Four- or five-star cool, at these prices."

"Glad you mentioned money. I'd think a man who

could afford this place could at least buy his wife a big diamond ring, don't you?"

"I do. But you'll have to talk to Uncle Maury about that, since he's footing the bill. I used some of that cash he gave me yesterday to pay for our room, so technically he's your man."

That wasn't the answer she wanted, so she went fishing again. "Still, I feel naked without a wedding ring. It's like we're living in sin."

Joe's chuckle teemed with innuendo. "Not yet we aren't. But just say the word, baby."

That was more like it. Still, Meg primly tilted her chin up, pretending to ignore his very pleasing comeback. "Anyway, it was nice of Maury to pay for the room."

"Crazy old dude, huh? His heart's as big as Texas. Although I still can't believe he's sticking to the Mafia story. I wonder why he gets so worked up if we say we're coming home?"

We're coming home. Such a domestic sentiment, one that struck a chord with Meg. "Right now it just seems easier to let him have his way."

"Can't complain in these surroundings. Being here with you isn't so bad, either."

Joe's languid, grinning expression melted Meg's bones.

"I saw a sign in the lobby announcing a wedding here tonight. That must be something to see."

Mindful of her pretty designer drink in one hand, Meg excitedly drew her knees up like a giddy teenager contemplating an upcoming dance. "Oh, it is. It's so romantic. They perform them on the wide steps in the garden. And with the Gulf of Mexico and a blazing sunset behind them, it's just beautiful. I would love to get married like that." She paused, then sat up straighter. "Hey, you want to see the wedding?"

"No." Sprawled lazily in his chair, Joe finished his drink and rested the plastic cup on his stomach. "There might be a pro-wrestling match or a tractor-pull on TV, woman. A man wouldn't want to miss that."

Meg fished an ice cube out of her drink and lobbed it at him. It hit him in his chest. Unruffled, he picked it off his T-shirt and popped it in his mouth, winking at her as he crunched it up and swallowed. The action struck her as supremely sexy simply because it was Joe doing it.

"Anyway, we're not invited. We'd be crashing," he said.

"No, we wouldn't. Look up there, about ten floors up." Meg twisted around in her chair and pointed to a wing of the sprawling building. "See that rooftop balcony? It's attached to the banquet room, which will be open while they set up for the reception. We can watch from there. Pretty cool, huh? What do you say?"

Joe looked at her questioningly. "I'm almost afraid to ask—but you've done this before, haven't you?"

"No, I have not, Mr. Smarty-Pants. A girlfriend of mine got married here about a year ago and I saw people watching. She said couples are told when they book the hotel that they can't expect the hotel's other guests to remain completely out of sight. But everyone was respectful. It was nice. So, what do you think? Want to do it?"

Joe raised an eyebrow. "You'll have to be more specific about what you mean by 'do it.'"

Secretly thrilled with his verbal foreplay, Meg

made a *tsk-tsk* sound. "I mean watch the wedding. Do you want to?"

"I don't know. You won't get all mushy and cry, will you?"

"I might. Will you?"

"Yes, but only if I have to buy them a gift."

"Like we know where they're registered. So?"

He shrugged. "Why not? It's better than running from imaginary hit men."

"Good." Having won her way, Meg sat back in her chair. "But they weren't imaginary this morning when they were banging on the door." She sipped her drink and worked the straw around in the ice. "You know, I keep thinking—"

"What if you're right, my great-uncle's not nuts, and they're for real?"

Meg nodded. "Exactly. Makes you wonder when they might catch up to us again." She looked around surreptitiously. "Or who might be sitting around us right now, doesn't it?"

"Nope." Joe settled back in his chair, appreciatively surveying their surroundings. "I haven't even spared them a thought until now. Why should I? I've got the sun, a beach, a pretty girl and a drink. Life is good."

"Great. I came in third. I must be slipping."

Joe rolled his head until he was looking into her eyes. "Don't flatter yourself. I was talking about the girl on the other side of me."

Meg sat up and peered around Joe. The deck-chair next to him was empty. He'd got her good, but Meg refused to rise to the bait. "I hate to tell you, cowboy, but I think someone let the air out of your date over there and she flew away."

"What?" Showing exaggerated surprise, Joe pivoted to look and then turned to Meg. The corners of his mouth twitched with humor but he managed to keep a straight face. "Damn, and I just bought that at the gift shop, too."

"As if." Meg rudely, loudly, finished off her drink.

"Hey, you, those slurping noises mean it's all gone."

"Oh. In that case…" She set the tall plastic glass in the sand, knowing someone from the hotel's poolside bar would come around momentarily to pick it up. "You know, Joe, you're not half-bad—mood-wise—once you get your coffee and shower in the morning."

He nodded, also putting his cup in the sand. "I smell better, too."

"I noticed that, as well."

"Thanks." Chuckling, Joe closed his eyes against the afternoon sunlight.

Meg feasted her eyes on him. The man was so strikingly handsome, it just hurt. Lying back in the chair, he looked like a Greek god sculpted in a reclining pose. He didn't lose a thing in profile, either. High cheekbones. Patrician nose. Wide, sensual lips and a strong jawline. She watched as a gentle breeze lifted his sandy-colored hair off his forehead.

"Joe?"

"Yes?" He didn't move a muscle or open his eyes.

"I was just wondering, and it's really none of my business—"

"But?" He knitted his fingers together atop his abdomen.

"But…are you going to call Linda back?"

Though he kept his eyes closed, a fine tension settled at the corners of his mouth. "Can't stand suspense, huh?"

"No. Not really."

"What about Carl?"

"Please. I'm in no hurry to call him. But knowing him, he's already out with someone else while he waits for my answer."

"Men are such slime."

"I know. Lucky for me and my heart, though, I really don't care about him. So, what about you, Joe?"

"I don't care about Carl, either."

Meg chuckled. "Silly. I meant, what about Linda?"

He finally looked over at her. "Well, it's a little harder to call her now that my cell phone's lost its charge."

"I have the same problem with mine."

"Too bad Uncle Maury didn't bring the chargers along with our underwear and toothbrushes. And I can't use the hotel phone. Linda has caller ID and would not be amused to see some hotel's name and number pop up when I'm supposed to be staying with my uncle. That's trouble I don't need right now."

"No, I guess not." How depressing. He remained concerned about Linda's feelings. Sure, it was admirable. But the obvious leap to a conclusion here was he would only care if he were still thinking about being with her. For the sake of the conversation, Meg threw out her two cents' worth. "You could press star sixty-seven, if you really wanted to talk to her. That blocks your location."

"A surefire way to raise a woman's curiosity."

Suddenly grumpy over all this solicitous care Joe was taking of Linda's stupid feelings, Meg blurted,

"God, you can't even go to a beach hotel with a relative while you're on vacation in Florida? For all she knows that's exactly what you did. Is she always so suspicious?"

"No. But you have to admit she has every reason to be, after my conversation with her this morning. And I can't tell her I'm here with Uncle Maury. What if she wants to talk to him? Or calls him at the house later, and he answers?"

"Who's to say she hasn't already done that? Maybe she thought she should apologize for hanging up on you earlier—"

Joe sat bolt upright. "Oh, damn, I didn't even think about that."

Meg reached over and put a hand on his arm. "Calm down. If she'd called, Maury would have covered for you and then let you know. And that hasn't happened, as far as we know. So no big whoop."

Joe stared fixedly as he apparently considered the logic of Meg's scenario. Then he relaxed and nodded. "Yeah, you're right. He'd cover for me."

As Joe settled back into his chair, Meg fought a grin that threatened to turn into a laugh. "You're afraid of her, aren't you?"

Indignation thinned Joe's lips to a straight line. "I am not."

"You are so. What is she—jealous for a living or something?"

"No. I just don't want to make things any harder for her than they're already going to be. Which may be tough. She's not usually suspicious, but she does stay on top of things."

"Really? Like what?"

"Mountains, mostly."

"As in making them out of molehills?"

"Actually, she's a ski instructor at a Colorado resort her family owns. She's also training for the Olympics, so she doesn't need anything distracting her focus right now, either."

"Dear God, all that? She's also blond, isn't she?"

"What does that have to do with it?"

"Isn't she, Joe?"

"Yes."

"Oh, who didn't know?" Picturing what this rich paragon of athletic vitality and, no doubt, Swedish good looks must be like, Meg said levelly, "I think I hate Linda."

Joe grinned. "A lot of women do."

"So, what does she do when there's no snow?"

Joe looked almost apologetic. "She's working on a master's in creative writing. She wants to write about her experiences teaching skiing to the disabled."

Meg gripped her chair's arms. "Oh, man, the Mother Teresa of the slopes. Is there no end to this woman? Tell her to save some for the rest of us. And you—why haven't you married her yet, Joe? Even I'm considering it."

He laughed. "I'll pass that on to her. But tell me, Meg, how do you think I should handle this whole Linda thing?"

Cut her up in little chunks and feed her to the sharks was Meg's first thought, which she did not voice. "Sorry, cowboy. That's not my call to make."

"Ha-ha, your call to make. I get it." He turned his face up to the sun. "What does it matter, anyway? I'm thinking of moving here."

Meg's heart did happy somersaults. "You mean to Florida? Really?"

"Sort of. I meant to this very beach. This exact spot. Just squat here and become a beach bum."

"Oh." Disappointed, Meg stretched her legs out in front of her. "You wouldn't be the first one who did. You think Linda would like being a beach bum, too? Or bum-ette, I suppose."

"No, I don't think she would. She loves the mountains."

"Yeah, it'd be kind of hard to snow ski without them. Hey, maybe you could build her some sand mountains here on the beach and a castle atop them. I bet she'd like that."

"Enough about Linda." Joe gave her one of his slow, sexy grins as his expression warmed. "How about you, Meg? Would you like some guy to build you a sand castle on the beach and put you in it?"

His intense gaze, with eyes as blue as a mountain lake, robbed Meg's bones of strength. She swallowed hard and strove for nonchalance. "Depends on the guy. And the castle."

"Really?" In one fluid motion, Joe sat up and swung his legs over the side of the wooden chair. Leaning toward her, he held a hand out, obviously wanting her to take it.

Meg eyed his hand and then him. "What are you doing?"

"I have a sudden urge to build a sand castle. Do you want to go with me and see what we can make together?"

Meg's breath caught in her throat. His offer sounded, though she really knew better, like an off-beat proposal. She could barely meet his gaze as she slipped her hand into his strong capable one. "Yes...I do."

THAT EVENING, freshly showered and dressed casually—as befitted the ogling of the wedding of two strangers to him—in lightweight denims and a clean salmon-colored knit shirt, Joe stood in front of the mirror mounted on the back of the closed bathroom door and combed his hair. As he did, he tried very hard not to picture Meg on the other side of this very door, maybe still naked from her shower.

"Get a grip," he muttered in warning to himself. "Think about Linda, man. Don't mess this up."

But it was already messed up even more than when he'd headed to Florida to think about the two of them. Everything had changed in the past twenty-four hours, and it was all Meg's fault, Joe concluded benignly as he tucked his comb back into his pocket.

So, what was this thing that was brewing with her? Clearly, something was. She felt it, too—otherwise he wouldn't have a fond memory of her lifting the covers last night to check him out. Sure, she'd captured his attention on all levels—he already felt as if he'd known her for years, and she was warm and intelligent and funny, everything you'd want a person to be—but, wow, the sexual chemistry between them was incredible.

Massaging his forehead with his fingertips, Joe slowly exhaled. Meg made him feel like he was seventeen again—one big walking hormone. *Oh, baby.* If she had any idea of his runaway erotic thoughts of her, she'd spend her day slapping his face over and over. And he would deserve it. But the hard truth was, he couldn't act on that desire. Well, he could. So could she. All they had to do was admit what they felt, jump in bed and go for it. Just do it.

Joe exhaled slowly to get himself under control. Another few seconds of thoughts like that and he'd be using a chair to batter down the door between them. Wouldn't she be surprised? And wouldn't he be arrested.

Okay, maybe not. What if he just came on to her? What would she do? Accept? He pretty much thought so. But would it be worth it? Hell, yes, sexually it would.

But what about afterward? Could they—in the most serious sense of the cliché—respect themselves or each other the next morning? Wouldn't he be shot through with guilt for cheating on Linda? And wouldn't Meg think, *If you can cheat on her so easily, then will you eventually cheat on me, too?* Talk about a solid basis for building distrust—and Meg already had a boatload of that for Carl because of his cheating. But what about Meg herself? No one had to tell Joe that she wouldn't relish being the "other woman" to Linda, or any other woman. Ever. So, to be with Meg, he'd have to first make a clean break with Linda.

He knew what he wanted—needed—to say to Linda. He just hated like hell to do it over the phone. What he had to say was best and honorably said face-to-face. That was how he'd want her to handle it if the situation were reversed. So, until he went home and saw her, she and he were still a couple, at least in her heart. That meant he'd better not talk to her before then—even to apologize for this morning—because everything he said would be a dodge or a lie.

A frown of distaste claimed Joe's features as he gazed at his reflection in the mirror. "Joe, my man," he said, "the woman on the other side of this door has turned your life upside down in one big hurry."

"Did you say something, Joe?" Meg called out.

Caught, he laughed. "Yeah, I said I wonder what you look like naked."

"Ha. Wouldn't you like to know."

"Wasn't that what I just said?"

"Maybe, but don't even think about coming in here." From her side of the door, she fiddled with the lock, obviously testing it.

Chuckling, Joe growled like a big, bad wolf and rattled the doorknob, which made Meg shriek. He knocked gently on the door. "Hey, you…just kidding." Like hell he was. For two cents, he'd forget his damned cowboy-gentleman code of honor and— "If you don't hurry, Meg, we're going to miss out on the wedding. And I will have wasted all this time making these water balloons out here."

"Water balloons? You did not."

"Did, too."

"Did not." A pause. "But wouldn't that be funny?"

"Unless you were in the wedding party. Or with hotel security."

"True. I won't be much longer. I had to wash my hair twice to get all that sand out. Give me five minutes to finish up, okay?"

"Yes, ma'am," he said to her, and then added quietly to himself, "It's like we're married."

He started to move away from the door, but the

notion of marriage stopped him cold. Not because it freaked him out and made him want to run, like it had with Linda. But because it didn't. *Huh. Me and Meg. Or Meg and I. The two of us…playing house. Or castle, I guess.* A grin tugged at Joe's lips as he leaned a shoulder against the bathroom doorjamb. His thoughts, like a videotape inserted into a VCR, did a quick rewind back to their afternoon antics on the beach. Though they'd had more fun than two five-year-olds, the result of all their efforts—a sand castle—had not measured up.

Apparently it was true that time and tide wait for no man. Or woman. Frantically, they'd tried to hold back the water and save their masterpiece. But in the end, Mother Nature had won out, using her ocean's relentless waves to batter their creation into more of a melting lump of goo than a fairy-tale vision of happily-ever-after.

Thinking of fairy-tale endings carried Joe across the room to the big picture window that gave them the much-coveted water view. And it was gorgeous: the foamy turquoise ocean, the eggshell-colored sand, the tanned couples strolling leisurely along the beach, the shell seekers bent over their finds, and the lowering sun smiling benignly over it all. A man could be happy here…with Meg.

Joe chuckled fatalistically. "I am in trouble."

Until yesterday, until Meg, he'd just about concluded that Linda was the one for him—as any sane man would, if a woman like her even looked twice at him. But then along came this cute, funny, little, dark-haired third-grade teacher from Florida who just knocked his damned socks off with one look.

Just blew him right out of the saddle—something Linda, despite her stunning looks, personality and wealth, had never been able to do.

Joe sobered with the realization that he was going to have to hurt Linda. Damn, that didn't feel good. He crossed his arms over his chest and rocked back on his heels. If only she were not so damned nice, what he had to tell her would be easier. But she was—smart and nice. She gave to charity and volunteered her time with the less fortunate. The woman was a paragon of—

"Joe?"

He pivoted to see Meg standing just inside the bedroom. His breath caught in his suddenly dry throat. "Wow." What had happened to his funny little dark-haired schoolteacher? In her place was a beautiful woman of peaches-and-cream skin, shining auburn hair that fell past her shoulders, and wide, brown eyes. He grinned at her. "You sure do clean up nice, ma'am."

"Thanks, cowboy. So do you. You like my dress, then?"

"Oh, I'm sorry. You're wearing a dress?"

She put her hands to her waist. "Is that supposed to be a compliment?"

"Absolutely. But, sure, I like your dress. It's nice." To Joe, it was a rust-colored, sleeveless thing that came to her knees. That was the extent of his women's-fashion knowledge. "What I like more is what you do for your dress."

Very primly but looking pleased, she smoothed her hands down the front of her outfit. "Thank you. I forgive you."

Joe grinned. "Whew. Dodged that bullet. Still, I've got to hand it to my uncle—he sure knows how to pack a woman's bag for her, even on the fly."

"I'll give him that. But I would still like to know how he got into my apartment."

"Me, too." Joe marveled at how he could manage to talk sensibly while the very sight of her filled his vision and overwhelmed his senses. "Uncle Maury really had no right to invade your privacy. But my guess—after his showing up in our hotel room this morning—is that he gave your landlord twenty bucks."

"Ha. Not Mrs. Warden. That's her real name, too, and she looks just like one. He didn't get past her, trust me. It's more likely Maury has a set of lock picks."

"Wouldn't surprise me in the least." Joe patted himself down, checking for the room key and his wallet. "So, you ready to go? Although, I really shouldn't take you because you'll outshine the bride."

Meg raised her chin in the teasing gesture Joe was coming to recognize. "Still, I bet the bride has a big diamond ring to show off, *Mr. Smith*."

"I'm sure she does, *Mrs. Smith*." Joe walked over to her and took her arm to escort her out of the room—before his baser instincts could win out and have him tearing off her clothes and throwing her on the bed, hopefully to her delight. "But, then again, I suspect the bride puts out."

With that, Joe opened the door that led into the hallway—and Meg said, "Well, I can put out, too, if there's a ring and a long, white dress in it for me. I didn't know that was all it takes."

Joe froze with his hand on the doorknob. In the next instant, he pulled her back inside the room and allowed the door to close behind them. He gathered her in his arms and held her gaze with his. "Meg Kendall, though I have no right to, and though I've been giving myself all sorts of speeches while you were getting ready about doing the right thing, I am now going to kiss you so hard you'll bruise."

"Really? Where exactly?" She wrapped her warm, bare arms around his neck and grinned up into his face.

Joe exhaled roughly. "Do you have any idea what you do to me? Do you know how hard it is—"

"I think I do." She pushed herself seductively against him. "That is, unless you have a gun stuffed down your pants—a rather large-caliber gun, too, I might add." She raised her eyebrows appreciatively. "You go, boy."

By now, the ability to speak had left Joe. All he could do was stare at her.

Meg laughed teasingly. "Joe, are you all right? Do I need to pinch you?"

The sound of her voice brought him back to earth. "No. And thanks for saying that about my...gun's caliber. But what I meant was, being in hotel rooms with you, and feeling for you what I do, and not being able to act on it...well, do you know how hard that is?"

Looking smug and sexy, she said, "No. Tell me."

Joe ran his hands down her rib cage to her waist and rested them there. "I'd rather show you."

"Then...show me."

"Seriously? Right now? What about the wedding?" Dumb question. Showed how much blood was *not* going to his brain.

Meg chuckled. "Forget the wedding. Let's play honeymoon."

Joe's breath caught. "Are you sure, Meg, really? I mean, with everything going on—"

"Joe, this is my invitation. Are you telling me no?" She'd pulled back in his arms to look into his eyes. "Well?"

He gave up trying to reason. "Not only 'No, I'm not,' but 'Hell no, I'm not.'"

With that, he lowered his head to capture her mouth. A spark of honest-to-God electricity shocked his lips when they met hers. He fought to hold back, fearing he really would bruise her, so powerful was his lust for her. And that was exactly what it was—lust, a primal drive beyond mere desire, a pure need like he'd never known existed.

All he heard were her sweet moans. All he could feel was her body molded to his, her heart beating in time with his, her breasts hard against his chest, his hardness throbbing against her belly, his hand cupping her chin, molding her mouth to his, her hands clutching at his shirt. All Joe could think was—

He broke their kiss and pulled back. His mouth was wet with her kiss, his body screamed for oneness with hers, and he was breathing as if he'd just won a marathon. "Meg, I don't have any condoms. None."

Meg was breathing like she'd come in second in that same marathon. "Well, get some. Do it now, Joe. Call Room Service."

"Room Service?" His breathing eased a bit, but still he held onto her arms. "I don't think condoms are something they serve on a tray, if you get my drift. How about Housekeeping?"

"Not even. Do you see them sending some sweet little maid around to a guy who's just put in a request to have condoms sent to his room? Besides, do you really want to tell some woman on the phone what kind and how many?"

"You're right. Thirty minutes after that phone call I'd be down at the police station having my mug shot taken. Okay, you wait here. I'll go down to the gift shop—"

"I'm going, too."

"Aw, jeez, not this again." Joe let go of her and put his hands to his waist. "Seriously? You want to go help me buy condoms? You want to be standing there while I pick up a box and take it to the register?"

"Hardly. I'll be in another aisle, pretending to look at…souvenirs or candy bars or something."

Joe's ardor began wilting. "Candy bars. Why can't you just wait here, Meg? It makes more sense—"

"What if the Mafia shows up while you're gone?"

"Up here or downstairs?"

"Either way. And don't act like they're not after us and like Maury is crazy or this is a game. I think we both know better."

"No we don't. I haven't accepted that at all. But if they are on our trail, how would we recognize them? The first *hit men* we saw turned out to be partying Goths. And the second batch ended up being my great-uncle, with his black socks and sandals, and probably a couple of his cronies we never saw."

"Maybe. But Maury told us to stay together. So, while you're shopping, I can keep a watch out for big, muscled, dangerous-looking guys dressed in black and who have guns and broken noses."

"Do you hear yourself? This isn't *The Godfather*, Meg. They won't be that obvious."

"How do you know?"

Well, she had him there. "You're right. I don't. Come on, then." He took her hand and pulled her out of the room with him, intent on finding the gift shop, and a big box of condoms with their names on it.

8

WHILE KEEPING a surreptitious eye on Joe, Meg had pored over the selection of magazines. Considered every candy bar. Read every refrigerator magnet. Checked out the romance novels. She'd even tried on three or four pairs of sunglasses. And now, with nothing else left to do in the tiny shop, she intended to rummage through a shelf of folded cotton sweaters, all bearing the hotel's name and logo. To do this, she made polite "excuse me" noises and stepped around two women with bored-looking teenage daughters in tow.

Once in front of the garments, Meg found the stack that was her size and made a selection. Holding the sweater up to her, she turned around and looked down at herself, ostensibly to check the effect. She then pretended to be looking for her husband to get his opinion.

Joe stood about two aisles away. Visible only from the chest up, he wore a frown of concentration on his face worthy of a scientist trying to split an atom.

Meg sighed, thinking it was a good thing Joe was really hot and a great kisser, because he could be exasperating. What the heck was he doing? How much concentration did he need to buy a box of condoms?

Surely he'd done this before—and in less than the ten minutes it had already taken him to study the display. Meg was left to wonder how big a selection the hotel carried. And why.

Just then, Joe looked up and around. Clearly he was looking for her, so Meg subtly cleared her throat. Joe caught sight of her and held up—*held up!*—two different boxes, one in each hand, for her to see. Some patrons of the small gift shop noticed, too, and looked from Joe to her and back…and grinned. Others looked appalled and left. Instant mortification burned Meg's cheeks. Aghast, she frowned and shook her head, mouthing, *What the hell are you doing?*

In answer, Joe held one box out toward her and mouthed something like *Ribbed thins for your pleasure*. He pulled it back and held out the other box, mouthing *Lubricated for your comfort*. He shrugged to indicate his indecision.

Meg could have died right there on the spot. The man was insane, just like his great-uncle. Someone tapped her on the shoulder, making her jump about a foot. But it was only a thin, ancient, white-haired lady in a flowered, hot-pink muumuu who smiled and said, "Tell him to get both, honey."

Meg felt ill. "I beg your pardon?"

"I said, tell him to get both kinds."

"I don't—"

"Of course you do. Listen, if that good-looking young man waving those condoms around over there wanted my body, *I'd* tell him to get both boxes."

She'd said this last bit loudly enough that everybody else in the store heard it. Two teenage girls perked up, their incensed mothers tried to hustle them away, and a young father, with two kids in tow, wistfully eyed the condoms Joe held up. Whether he was fondly remembering sex, or wished now that he'd used condoms when he had engaged in the act, Meg had no idea. Her response, however, was knee-jerk.

"I don't know what you're talking about, ma'am. I've never met that man before in my life. Here—" she pushed the sweater she held into the startled older woman's hands "—this will look great on you with your coloring and your…pink muumuu."

With that, Meg hustled away from the woman, wanting to get out of the store as soon as possible.

But Joe had no intention of being left behind, apparently. He called even more attention to her by shouting, "Meg! What's wrong? Where're you going?"

She didn't stop, didn't turn around, didn't acknowledge that she knew him. But there was plenty she wanted to say. *Ribbed or lubricated. As if. Just make a stupid decision. How hard can it be? I mean, really. Who—other than that great-grandma lady who should know better—cares what kind?*

Finally away from the scene of her humiliation, Meg rushed headlong for the elevator bank, praying one would be there, waiting to whisk her upward from this sub-lobby level of Hell and back to the real world. She rounded a final corner into a minuscule foyer, skirted a huge terra-cotta pot planted with a real palm tree—and ran smack into a big, muscled guy dressed all in black, his hair slicked back, who was just then exiting an elevator car. Also stepping out of the car behind him were two more guys just like him. All three men looked as startled as Meg was, but the one in the lead had grabbed her arms and was holding her tightly.

"Hey, whoa there. Where's the fire?"

Blind with fear, Meg stared up at him. How could she have allowed her embarrassment to drive her into the arms of the enemy? For that was exactly what she'd done—run away from Joe and right into the Mafia. Like some really stupid heroine in a poorly written book or movie. Meg did the only thing she could.

"I have pepper spray in my purse," she blurted.

Which was, at that very moment, unhelpfully stashed in the room—but no sense telling this guy with the Bronx accent that. It's not like she'd really use it, anyway.

The man who held her in place held up a hand, as if silently warning the two attack dogs behind him not to, well, attack. "I'm glad to hear you do. A lady needs protection. But I don't think there's going to be any call for that here."

"Let her go." This came from somewhere behind Meg. It was Joe and he sounded awfully serious.

Only, the Mafia guy didn't obey. Instead, the very big, strong man, still maintaining his grip on her, raised his head until he stared, no doubt, right into Joe's eyes. "Who're you?"

"Who wants to know?"

The mountain of a man sized Joe up. "Rocco is all you need to know. Now answer my question. I asked you who you are."

Meg was silently praying. *Don't be stupid, Joe. Don't be some macho hero. Just tell the nice, no-doubt armed man who you are.*

"Joe Rossi, if it's any of your business."

"I'm making it my business. Now, here's another question for you, Mr. Joe Rossi. Who are you to this lady?"

Before Joe could reply, Meg found her voice…a low, croaky one, but still a voice. "He's my…husband."

The man settled his gaze on her. "Is that so? The guy in the pink shirt is your husband?"

"Yes. And it's salmon…not pink. His shirt, I mean."

"Yeah, okay. So, what'd he do?"

She swallowed hard. "With what?"

"I don't know with what. To upset you. What'd he do?"

"Look, why don't you just leave her alone?" This was Joe and he sounded closer. "Your quarrel isn't with her. I'm the one who has The Stogie, and I'll show you right to the car right now, whatever you want. Just let her go."

The Mafia man frowned at Joe "That's all very interesting, Joe. Thanks." He looked down at Meg. "Does he always say crazy things nobody knows what he's talking about?"

Her shrug was necessarily a very subtle movement, clamped as she was in the guy's viselike grip. "A lot more than you'd think."

"I can believe that. So, again, what'd he do?"

"Well, he was in the little shop back there and trying to pick out some—" *Why was she telling him this?* "Nothing, really. He just embarrassed me. I don't think he meant to."

Meg was beginning to doubt this guy was Mafia. He talked more like some concerned citizen stepping in to make sure she wasn't being abused by her boyfriend or husband. How nice. And noble. She ventured a smile for him.

He returned it, showing her perfectly white and even teeth set in what was—she now noticed—a ruggedly handsome face. "You sure you're okay?"

"She's fine," Joe said testily.

"I'm not asking you," Rocco said, jutting his jaw out pugnaciously. Behind him, his two clones made threatening noises and shifted their weight impatiently. "I'm asking the lady."

The lady started talking. "I'm okay. Really. In fact, we're getting ready to go to a wedding. And then we're going out to eat. And then I think we'll take a moonlight walk on the beach." She was babbling, she knew it, but she couldn't stop herself. "We built a sand castle today, only the tide ruined it and I got a lot of sand in my hair and had to wash it twice, like it says on the bottle. I've never had to do that before."

Initially, the man was silent as he stared down at her. No doubt he wondered if she was insane or simple-minded. Looking uncertain, he released her and stepped back. "Your…hair looks real nice, Meg. I like it. In fact, I like you. And I wouldn't want anything bad to happen to you."

Relieved, Meg pressed a hand over her heart. "Neither would I, but thank you, you're very kind."

Joe stepped up, took hold of her elbow and tugged her as he stepped back to allow the three men to pass.

"Joe," she whispered as they moved away, tugging on his shirt to get his attention.

Tearing his challenging glare away from the departing men, he finally looked at Meg.

"I didn't tell that man my name."

Disbelief replaced his consternation. "What? Well, should I get him back so you can also give him your room number?"

"Shh. Lower your voice." Meg could have pinched him hard. "I don't want him to have my room number, goose. I'm saying the man *said* my name just now. He called me Meg."

Joe stared blankly at her, then realization dawned. "He did? You're sure you didn't tell him what it was?"

"Why in God's name would I do that? You told him yours, but I never said what mine was. Do you know what this means?"

"Yes," Joe said emphatically, but instantly changed his answer to "No, I don't. Maybe he heard me calling out to you from the shop. That has to be it. And, why did you run out of the store? What'd that elderly lady in the muumuu say to you?"

Meg's temples suddenly throbbed. "That is so *not* the point right now, Joe. But…she told me to tell you to buy both boxes, if you can believe that."

"She did? Well, sorry. When you ran out, I threw them down and…didn't buy any."

"You know what? I don't think it matters anymore. *However*—" she said pointedly "—that big, bad guy couldn't have heard you call out my name because he was still on the elevator when you did."

"Hmm." Joe looked from her to the men quietly disappearing down the long carpeted hallway and then back to her. "Are you sure, Meg? Really sure?"

"Oh, for—" She reached up and cupped his cheeks in her palms, forcing him to look into her eyes. "I'm sure I did not give that man my name. But more importantly, what are we going to do about it?"

"Hey, Rossi."

Meg froze, her eyes widened…a mirror image of Joe's expression. He pulled her hands away from his face. As one, they turned to the leader of the black-clad pack.

"Yeah?" Joe called out. Credit the man for sounding unconcerned and nonchalant.

"Tell Mr. Seeger he's only making things harder on himself, running like he is."

"Who says I know where he is to tell him anything?"

Rocco's grin had nothing to do with humor. "You know. Tell him I've got a message he needs to hear. It's about an old friend of his."

Putting an arm around Meg, Joe called back, "I don't take messages. Tell him yourself."

Meg jerked her head so fast in Joe's direction that her neck actually hurt. She whispered fiercely, "What are you doing? Have you lost your mind? Quit baiting him."

Joe spoke out the side of his mouth. "I'm not. Look at him. He doesn't know what to say now because I called his bluff. This is funny."

Meg's knees locked with the shock of it all. "No, it isn't. There are three of them, Joe. Any one of them is bigger than both of us together. And they have guns."

"No, they don't."

"Yes, they do. They're the Mafia. What do you think they have? Whistles and gumballs?"

"Come on, Meg, they're not Mafia. Yeah, there for a few minutes, I thought they might be. But when they didn't take The Stogie when I offered it, or take the two of us hostage—"

"You mean right here in front of all these people

coming and going from the shops? Just snatch us right out of this hallway in plain sight of everyone? I'd think—I'd hope—they'd be more polished than that, Joe."

"Good God, you have this whole thing romanticized, don't you? Come on, Meg, if these guys were the real deal, I'm betting we'd already be dead."

"Well, don't sound so happy about it."

"I'm not. I'm just saying they could have used us to flush Uncle Maury out of hiding. Yet they're not even interested—I don't even think it occurred to them. And they're letting me push them around, pretty much. So, isn't it obvious? If nothing else, how do you think Mr. Slick Hair knew your name? Answer: my great and nutty uncle told him. See? This is a game."

"Joe, you have got to get over thinking that. For one thing, it's gone on too long. I mean, what would be the possible point of keeping us together another day? What's Maury trying to do?"

Joe stared at her as if she'd just pushed the wrong button at a missile silo. "Oh, man, that's it, Meg. You got it. Uncle Maury *wants* us together. That's why he set up this blind date and everything that's followed. This has nothing to do with money, senility, or the Mafia. It has to do with us. Me and you."

Frowning her confusion, Meg glanced the way of the Mafioso, who seemed content to let her and Joe have this whispering conversation while they waited. "Well, it does kind of make sense."

"Exactly. Look, my uncle likes you a lot. And I'm probably his favorite relative. But he doesn't like Linda. He thinks she's too perfect, and he doesn't

mean it in a nice way, either. Anyway, he's orchestrat-
ing events so we're together every second—until we
fall for each other."

"Oh, Joe, that's just a bit over the—"

"No, it isn't. Watch this." Before she could stop
him, Joe called out to the patiently waiting mobsters,
"You guys are good, I'll give you that. You've had us
really going now for about twenty-four hours, so
take a message. Tell my great-uncle we're on to him.
Tell him we're not running anymore. We're staying
right here. Tell him I said 'Game over.'"

To Meg's surprise, the three men in black traded
subtle but uncertain glances with each other. Then,
Rocco said, "Yeah, we'll do that when we catch up to
him. In fact, I want to say the same thing to him myself—nice try, only no cigar…if you get my drift. You
two kids enjoy your evening. We'll be around."

With that, the three men turned and continued on
their way toward the door to the parking garage.

ABOUT THIRTY MINUTES LATER, as sunset approached,
Joe stood with Meg among a loose cluster of several
curious onlookers, on the rooftop balcony that
opened off the reception-ready banquet room. Man,
he reflected, there was nothing like an encounter
with mobsters, fake or otherwise, to cool your jets. He
and Meg had yet to get past first base with each other.
By tacit agreement, after downing a quick, stiff drink
from the poolside bar, they'd proceeded directly to
the very public wedding.

Right now, the sweet smell of Meg's perfume filled
his senses with renewed longing as he leaned, along
with her, over the chest-high, thick stucco wall to

peer down at the wedding in progress. He had to admit he'd had his doubts earlier about how a wedding held outside at a hotel, on the beach, with strangers in shorts and bathing suits gawking at the bride, could be romantic. But he was won over. The alfresco setting, complete with improvised altar area, red-carpeted aisle between two long rows of padded folding chairs, and plenty of flowers everywhere, was breathtaking. Especially when the background was a gorgeous expanse of beach that led down to the sun-sparkled waters of the Gulf of Mexico.

It was a perfect evening, although Joe would have felt better if he'd been able to reach Uncle Maury by phone. He told Meg he wasn't that concerned, figuring the old guy was purposely incommunicado, now that his friends had told him, no doubt, of their accidental encounter. Joe supposed he and Meg could go home now, but she hadn't mentioned doing so. And he wasn't about to. If she wanted to be here with him on this idyllic evening, then, by God, he wanted her to be, too.

"Oh, Joe—look," Meg whispered excitedly, pointing over the balcony's wall. "The bridesmaids are coming."

Joe peered over the side. And there they were. Three pretty women, doing that curious half-step walk unique to female participants in a wedding, strolled down the aisle to the accompaniment of canned but nonetheless inspiring music. They wore wide-brimmed hats and their gowns were mint-green and lacy. They had to hate those dresses. Joe knew this from everything he'd ever heard from his sister, her friends and various of his girlfriends about how they always hated bridesmaids' dresses because they were expensive, couldn't be worn to anything else ever again and always reminded the wearer that she wasn't the bride.

"You know what I just thought of?" Meg said, turning to him, her voice lowered respectfully. "My best friend Wendy's younger sister's wedding is tonight, too, in Dallas. I can't believe it. Here we are, whole states apart, but both at weddings that aren't ours." She sighed.

"Yeah, I know how you feel," Joe said, sounding disappointed. "It's not my wedding, either. I just hate that."

"Oh, I bet you do, you poor thing." She moved in closer to him.

Joe put an arm around her, resting his hand possessively on her shoulder. She smiled up into his face. "I just love weddings."

"Yeah…me, too," he whispered next to her ear, delicately kissing her hair.

She pulled back to run her gaze over his face. "Do you really? Are you just saying that? Guys hate weddings. They act like wild stallions that have just been roped and tied—"

"Preparatory to being gelded. Yeah, that's our official stance, the one in the manual." She elbowed him in the ribs, causing him to wince. "But I was going to add that if this wedding makes you want to cuddle with me, then I'm all for it." Affectionately squeezing her shoulder, he grinned at her.

Her face colored prettily as she ducked her head and turned her attention back to the procession below. The music swelled…. "Here comes the bride!" Meg blurted. "Oh, isn't she beautiful? Look at that dress. And her flowers. Oh...and her hair—I love her hair—"

"Shh, Meg," Joe whispered. "People are staring at you."

Meg stiffened with horror and, pulling away from him, started edging away from the wall. "Oh my God, I do not *believe* this."

When she tried to tug him back with her, Joe, amused, resisted. "Hey, it's okay. I don't think they heard you down there. It's like ten floors below."

"Not that," she whispered, pointing in the direction of the wedding scene below. "Look down there, but do it carefully. The third row on the left, about halfway in. Tell me if my eyes are deceiving me."

"What's going on, Meg? Am I going to see those goons from before? Because I told you I don't think they're—"

"Oh, I wish it was them." She shoved him toward the balcony's solid wall. "Go ahead. Look."

"Okay, okay. Quit pushing." Joe peered over the wall, quickly locating the spot. So what was the big deal? Wedding guests. A whole row of them. He'd expected maybe to see his great-uncle right in the thick of things. But...no. Confused now, Joe turned to Meg—and she wasn't there. He looked around, muttering, "What the hell?"

Finally he spotted her, standing back from the wall, almost to the striped awning that shaded the far half of the balcony. Standing rigidly, her very pretty features now a mask of rank disapproval, she signaled desperately for Joe to hurry to her. "What—or who—exactly am I looking for, Meg? Because I don't recognize—"

"Carl," she hissed. "It's Carl, Joe. Here. At the wedding. With a date."

Joe didn't bother pointing out to her that since he had no idea what Carl looked like—and still didn't, except maybe for the top of his head—he couldn't have verified for her what her eyes were showing her. But smartly taking the high road here, he said, "The man is slime."

"I told you he is. He never mentioned anything to me about having a wedding to go to, and we only broke up a week ago."

"Maybe the bride or the groom is her friend and he just met this woman—"

"Are you really going to take his side, Joe? Really?"

"I'm not taking sides. I—"

"He has his arm around that woman. Did you see that part? Didn't I tell you he was a jerk? Do you see what I mean?" Her voice was rising, not in volume but in octaves. "I haven't even turned down his marriage proposal yet."

"Shh, it's okay, Meg. You don't even like him, remember?"

"Oh, I remember. And now you can see why. He's a big, fat cheater. And did you see that woman? Some blonde with big hair and a big chest. It's not Linda, is it? Wouldn't that be the perfect irony?"

"Irony wouldn't even begin to cover it. But I'm pretty sure it's not Linda," he said, his voice conciliatory. "Maybe that woman's not his date. Maybe she's his sister."

That helpful little comment earned him a scathing

look. "He doesn't have a sister. He's a spoiled only child."

"Then I say we kill him."

Meg raised an eyebrow. "Good idea." She pivoted to her right and headed for the open French doors that led into the banquet room.

Alarm shot through Joe. He had visions of her interrupting the wedding down below, beating Carl to death with a folding chair and then saying in court, during her trial, that it was all Joe Rossi's idea. He took off after her, catching her by the arm as she passed over the threshold into the building. "Wait a minute, Meg. What are you going to do?"

She jerked her arm out of his grip. "I'm going to kill him, just like you said."

And there it was—his worst nightmare. Joe glanced around the suddenly quiet room, seeing a number of eyes looking back at them. Amazing how that many people could be so suddenly still and attentive. Standing in a sea of white-cloth-covered and flower-bedecked tables with mint-green accents everywhere, Joe said to the room in general, "She's just kidding."

Meg said, "No, I'm not." She held out her hand to him. "Give me that knife you said you have."

A loud, nervous laugh erupted from Joe. "Such a kidder, this one. Come here, you."

His jaw set, Joe firmly grabbed her arm and marched her across the room. "If you'll forget murder, I promise you I will come up with something that will hit him where it hurts worst—right in the old love life. With any luck, it won't be something that gets us both thrown into prison for the rest of our lives."

"Prison? Oh my God, it's coming true. Wendy said I would end up there one day and have to be some big sweaty chick's bitch."

Joe performed a neat double take. "What?" Still hustling her out of earshot of the very interested waitstaff, he kept shooting her pointed, and amused, glances. "You know, I don't even have a response to that—except to say I think being in prison is enough punishment for a…big sweaty chick without tossing *you* into her cell. So let's just see if we can keep you out of there, all right?"

9

It was late now. Close to midnight. And what an evening it had been, Meg mused, reliving it all in quick, kaleidoscopic bursts of memory. The Mafia encounter and the Carl sighting had been so upsetting that Joe had suggested they abandon their idea to eat out and go for a moonlight walk on the beach instead. Sounded good to her. So they'd called Room Service and ordered two steak suppers with all the trimmings. While they'd waited for the food to arrive, they'd laughed about the chances of the Mafia or Uncle Maury showing up instead of Room Service.

But when their order had arrived in the care of a skinny, harmless guy named Roy, he'd received a hero's welcome and a big tip, much to his confused delight. They'd then eaten their supper right down to the T-bones, shoved the cart back out in the hall, ordered up an action-adventure movie on the TV, jumped on the bed like two kids and watched the show. And now here they were, just lying here with the TV on, not talking and totally avoiding the subject of sex and how they hadn't done it yet, despite their really, really wanting to earlier—before their ill-fated condom-buying trip.

Darn it. Had Joe cooled toward her? Was his mind

now full of thoughts of Linda? Was he sorry for what they'd done earlier…the kisses, the words of wanting?

The hard truth was he could be. If so, Meg didn't really want to know. What she'd like to do—but couldn't really see herself doing—despite her new-found boldness, was turn to him and say, *So, are you going to blow Linda off, like me better and have sex with me, or not? If the answer's yes, I'd be more than happy to hand you the phone right now so you can tell her to go jump off a mountain without her freakin' skis.* Wouldn't that be charming? Wouldn't it totally set the mood for something wild and wonderful between her and Joe? *Not.*

To make matters worse, or more frustrating, Joe was lying on the big, inviting bed with her, all kicked back with pillows propping him up. It just wasn't fair, all this masculine pulchritude and none of it hers. Why, the man could easily grace a building-size men's underwear ad in Times Square, he was so well put together. He was also so close she could smell his aftershave, which mingled sinfully with his own personal scent. Certainly, the whole physical package was there, but what she felt for him—the desire, the yearning—was way beyond that.

She'd known him less than thirty hours, and yet she already knew she wanted his nearness, the intimacy of him holding her and kissing her hair and telling her he cared. She wanted him to make her feel warm and safe and protected. She wanted everything with him, all the emotions and experiences she'd never had before with a man—and quite possibly couldn't have with this one, either. *Damn it.*

Or could she? After all, it'd be a shame to waste all this effort Maury had put into keeping them together—

Joe's most recent theory—by letting tonight slip away in innocence. Surely she should at least attempt to honor her sweet old neighbor's wishes by making an effort. Meg exhaled slowly, gathering her nerve.

Striving for nonchalance, she said, "So, that was pretty funny, huh, Joe?"

He hit the mute button on the remote control and turned to her. "What was?"

Her comment had earned her his steady regard. Oh, those blue, blue eyes of his with the sensual glint in them! She watched him roving his gaze slowly over her face, as if he needed to memorize each of her features for a future test. Meg could barely swallow. She subtly cleared her throat, prayed for speech to come to her lips again, and croaked out, "I'm sorry…what was…?"

He chuckled. "I don't know. That's what I was asking you. But I will say this—you have the best bedroom eyes I've ever seen. Like dark chocolate that melts in your mouth."

Well, she liked hearing that. "You got all that out of my eyes, cowboy?"

He nodded slowly. "That and more."

The man was wreaking havoc with her breathing. She stared mutely at him, seeing the unasked but burning question in his eyes. Unexpectedly, she felt shy.

"Do I make you nervous, Meg?" His bold, intent stare said he damn well knew he did and he wasn't sorry, either.

Neither was she. "Oh, yeah, you do…among other things."

"Good. So, you were trying to tell me something was funny?"

She opened her mouth, just enough to allow her to catch her breath against the fine tension invading her body. "I was?"

"You were."

"Oh. Yes." Mentally shaking herself out of her delicious lethargy, she sat up straighter, as if the very air was not humid and heavy with desire. "I meant you. You're funny. I cannot believe you crank-called Carl's room!"

That got a laugh out of him...a husky rumbling sound from deep in his throat. Meg practically had to sit on her hands to keep from placing them open-palmed on his chest just so she could feel the vibration. "Me, neither," he said. "Pretty immature, huh?"

"Maybe. But better than murder and prison—"

"Which comes with a big sweaty chick telling you you're her woman now."

"Amen." Dressed in cotton lounging short-shorts and matching T-shirt—Maury could be her mother, he'd packed so well for her—Meg sat propped up against pillows. "What a coincidence that Carl the cheater is staying here—"

"Soon to be *was* staying here."

"No doubt. It's just like him to book a room for Mr. and Mrs. Carl Woodruff. Ha! What an ego. He wouldn't even use a fake name like we did. He just wanted everyone to know he has a woman in his room. Well, who cares?"

Joe chuckled. "I bet the fake Mrs. Woodruff soon will. And not in a good way, either."

"I hear you. Once the wedding reception breaks up and they go to their room and pick up that message from the 'front desk' saying Carl's 'wife' called to tell him that she and the children could get away after all and that they would be driving down right now to join him, his big evening is so over. I just pray that he doesn't hear it first and delete it. Oh, I'd love to see his face while he's trying to explain it to his date. That big blonde will tear him a new one before he can say a word to defend himself."

Dressed in navy blue nylon athletic shorts and a T-shirt from the hotel's gift shop, Joe grinned. "Pretty brilliant, huh? Especially the part where I said there was something wrong with the hotel's phones and therefore his wife couldn't leave the message herself."

"You are fabulous, do you know that?" Giddy with the deliciousness of the gotcha Joe had perpetrated, Meg impulsively grabbed him around his neck and peppered his face with kisses as she praised him. "You are so brilliant, even going down to the pay phone in the lobby to make the call so it couldn't be traced to this room. How anonymous. How wonderful—"

"Whoa, ease up, woman." Joe held her arms and grinned at her. "Do you have any idea how much all your compliments are turning me on? Don't start something you're not ready to finish. That's the rule."

She froze, stared at him—and then scooted back over the sheets to her side of the bed. "I am so sorry. I wasn't thinking. I just got carried away with the moment—"

"Meg. It's okay. I enjoyed it."

"You did?"

"Of course I did. Why wouldn't I?"

"Are you serious? Do you really want me to start naming the people and reasons why you have every right to say you shouldn't?"

Making a face, Joe held up a cautioning hand. "Please don't. I know them all. Besides, I said why wouldn't I, not why *shouldn't* I."

"That's true." Meg's voice dragged with defeat. "But what do we do with that? The 'shouldn't' part, I mean. This is really confusing, Joe. Seriously, we both know what we feel for each other. At least, I think we do." She was taking a big chance here, but she forced herself to meet his gaze. "We do, right?"

Joe's chuckle had nothing to do with humor as he ran a hand through his hair and then massaged the back of his neck. "Yeah, we do, Meg," he finally said. "I don't think either one of us could deny it. And I'm not going to. Like you, I keep thinking about everything, and, well, it's pretty complicated in one way and really simple in another."

Meg restlessly shifted her position atop the bedcovers, finally sitting forward and crossing her legs like a kid sitting by a campfire. "You know what, Joe? We're talking all around this thing, so I'm just going to ask you what 'it,' specifically, you are talking about. Just so we're on the same page and don't end up embarrassing ourselves later."

"Fair enough. I guess I mean Linda. I keep thinking about Linda."

Disappointment filled Meg, but her laugh was self-deprecating, her humor a shield. "Wow. Shot down. You've been with me for nearly thirty solid hours and you *still* aren't sure you want to give up rich, blond, Miss World-Class-Perfect Linda? I must be losing it in the femme fatale category."

"I don't mean it that way, Meg. You're taking it wrong."

"Well, what's the right way to take it, then?" She'd pretty much snapped at him. "Sorry. That didn't come out like I wanted it to. I'm just frustrated."

"I know you are. Believe me, so am I. The good news is, we wouldn't be if we didn't, uh, feel something for each other, right?"

This was encouraging. "Right. So what do we do about it?"

"I can't—" Joe pressed his lips together, apparently against what he'd been about to say, and stared at her, looking uncertain how to proceed.

Meg shamelessly pressed the point. "You can't what?"

"I can't make a commitment to her, I guess."

With his first words, Meg's roller-coaster heart had soared to the heights—but by the end of his sentence had plummeted to the depths. "You guess? You really need to be sure about this, Joe. No guessing allowed."

"I wasn't guessing about how I feel. I was guessing that a commitment is what she is looking for from me. But, actually, it's much more serious than that."

"How serious?"

"Marriage serious."

"Yikes. But you don't...?" She dragged the word out, all the while shaking her head slowly as if to encourage him to answer in the negative.

"No. I don't."

Yes! It worked. Meg fisted her hand but stopped herself just short of pumping it victoriously in the air. Adopting a solemn expression, she continued as if she were the man's interested but uninvolved therapist. "I take it she asked you to marry her?"

"Yeah."

"And you…?"

"Took off for Florida."

Oh, good answer. "Whoa. So, do you think she's probably suspected what your answer is going to be? Like you told me about Carl, if I had to think about it, then the answer was always no—remember?"

"I do."

Meg got the irony of his reply right along with Joe, and laughed with him. "Better watch saying those two words, cowboy. They can get you into a lot of trouble."

The humor slowly left Joe's features. "I think I already am. A couple of days ago I was leaning toward telling Linda yes. But not anymore, Meg. I now know I would have been committing to her for all the wrong reasons, and she deserves better than that."

"So do you. But I think I know you well enough to say one of the reasons was never her money."

"No, it wasn't. And it's nice to know that comes through."

"In spades, Joe. You're very honorable. A man of conviction. I respect that."

He absently scratched at his temple. "You make me sound like I should run for sheriff."

Meg's eyes widened appreciatively. "Ooh, I think you'd look great in a uniform and a badge with a big old gun strapped to your hip, cowboy. Very sexy."

"Listen to you." Joe pulled a pillow out from behind his back and gave her a gentle whack with it.

Meg playfully fended off the feather-soft blow and slumped contentedly against her stack of pillows. "So, can I ask you something else?"

"Like I could stop you."

"True." She glanced over at him and inhaled for courage. "Okay, does your saying no to Linda... well, does it have anything to do with me, maybe?" A rush of embarrassed heat invaded her cheeks.

"Honey," he said, "it has everything to do with you in one way. And nothing at all to do with you in another."

"I wish I could say I know what you're talking about."

"What I meant was, on the one hand and independent of you, I came to realize that what I feel for Linda isn't everything it should be."

"Got that part." Meg crossed her legs and watched her foot waggling away nervously...or excitedly. "You, uh, said there was another part..."

Joe laughed at her. "You're on a fishing expedition, aren't you?"

She wouldn't look at him, just shrugged.

"All right, the other part is, I also realized that no matter how strong and real what I felt for Linda might have been...once I met you, it was all over. So I'm glad you came along when you did, because it would have caused a whole hell of a lot of heartache if I'd met you after I was already married."

Meg's heart brimmed with joy. "I don't know what to say."

Joe's raised eyebrows modeled alarm. "You better. Because if, after everything I just said, you say you only want to be my friend—"

"Joe, you and I could never be just friends."

"I know. And that's why, tomorrow morning, first thing, I'll call Linda and tell her it's over. I wanted to tell her face-to-face, but I don't think I can wait another week, or that she'll let me. I could fly back early and do it, but not in the middle of this Uncle Maury mess. So, bottom line, if I want any peace of mind, I have to call her." He sat up. "Maybe I should just call her right now—"

"Whoa, hold on, Joe." Meg placed a calming hand on his arm. "I appreciate your urgency, I really do. But don't call her tonight. Let her sleep. Tomorrow is plenty soon enough."

Relaxing, he slumped back against his pillows. "I guess you're right. And it's like you said, she probably knows it's coming."

Meg sat back, too, folding her hands together over her abdomen. "I think she does."

"And what about Carl?"

Meg grinned. "I think Carl's kind of busy right now, or I'd call him and tell him to bite me."

Joe grunted. "It shouldn't be so damn hard to do the right thing, should it?"

"No."

Joe was quiet for a moment and then softly said, "Hey, you."

Meg looked over at him to see the light dancing in his electric-blue eyes.

"I'm glad it's you, Meg. Glad as hell you came along when you did. You're amazing, and I want to get to know everything about you."

Happy tears caught her unaware and pricked at her eyes. Her smile trembled with emotion.

Joe sat up sharply and put a comforting hand on her thigh. "Hey, you're not going to cry, are you? Did I say something wrong? Just because I feel a certain way about you, Meg, it doesn't mean you have to feel it, too—"

"Oh, shut up, Joe." Leaning over to him, she gathered his hands in hers. "I feel the same way about you. It's crazy, but I've only known you one whole day and already we've been through so much that I feel as if we've known each other for years. You're so easy to be with and I really, really like you and you make me laugh and you're so freakin' hot—"

"Are you trying to seduce me, Meg?"

She stopped...and stared at him, wondering if, just like that, they were past the hard part and had truly moved on to the part where he was hard. No, that didn't sound classy. Maybe she should have said they were over the hump. And that didn't sound right, either. Okay, her mind was in the gutter. Or the bed. And Joe was still waiting for her answer.

Trying now to be nonchalant, she let go of his hands and tucked a lock of hair behind her ear. "Do you *want* me to seduce you?"

"Hell, yeah, I do."

Couldn't be more direct than that. Meg's mind whirled in great and happy circles, like a puppy chasing its tail. Suddenly, though, she remembered. "Well, great. What are we going to do? We don't have any condoms. And I'll bet that little drugstore in the sub-lobby is closed by now."

"Oh, do not be so quick to despair, my lady. Observe." Joe pinched up a fold of his hotel-logo T-shirt and held it taut. "Remember this? And me coming up with it in a bag after I made my phone call to Carl the jerk downstairs?"

"Yes. And how you didn't buy me anything."

"Sure I did. In a manner of speaking." He grinned from ear to ear.

It took Meg a second, but then she realized— "Oh my God!" Not sure if she was more embarrassed or titillated, she clapped her hands to her suddenly hot cheeks. "You did not!"

"Did so. Are you glad I did? Or are you going to slap my face because I did?"

"Glad. Definitely glad."

"Yes!" He twisted around to the nightstand on his side of the bed, opened the drawer and pulled out... "Ta-da! An entire box of thin-and-ribbed-for-your-pleasure-and-mine condoms."

Meg stared at the box and then at Joe. A silent, eager communication passed between them. "Oh, boyfriend!" Meg went up on her knees, grabbed the hem of her T-shirt and started pulling it up and over her head. "That's enough of talking and not touching. Get your clothes off, cowboy. You are about to get *so* lucky."

"Yee-haw!" Tossing the condom box down, Joe jackknifed to a sitting position and yanked his shirt over his head.

With that, "the first one naked wins" race was on.

JOE'S TOUCH WAS RIGHT for Meg from the first moment he put a hand on her bare skin. Lying on her side, facing him, with her eyes half closed, she gave herself over to the delicious sensation of his hands moving sensually over her body. Happily, there was no first-time awkwardness and no words necessary to tell him to touch her *here* or *like this*. This told her their actual coming together, when it happened, would be like a well-choreographed dance of two bodies, of two hearts, perfectly in tune with each other.

"Oh my God, Joe," she breathed dreamily as she roused herself enough to trail her fingertips down his clean-shaven cheek. "I knew it would be like this for us. I just knew it would be. You are so beautiful."

Smiling, he propped himself up on one elbow. With his other hand he lightly traced the curve of her body from shoulder to waist to hip and thigh...and back up her side. "I think I'm supposed to say that to you."

"Oh. Then go ahead."

"All right. Meg Kendall, I think you're beautiful and I have since I first saw your booty stuck in my face in that fitting room three days ago."

"Not that again," Meg moaned self-consciously. "I thought that was in the vault."

"It would be if I could get the image out of my mind." Without warning, Joe grabbed her—eliciting a squeal of surprised delight—and rolled onto his back, which meant she was happily stretched out, full-length and naked, atop him. Now his hands were everywhere...stroking, kneading, roaming.

Meg's breath came in tiny gasps of mounting desire as she lowered her head to capture his mouth in an eager, punishing kiss. With her elbows anchored against his pillow, she filled her fisted hands with his hair and pushed her body against his, mimicking the act itself.

His moan against her mouth and the ragged breathing through his nose like a bull preparing to charge told her she had him where she wanted him.

Finally, Joe broke their kiss and spoke, though he

could barely get words out. "Oh, man. I don't think I can wait, Meg."

Heated to the core with want for him, Meg tossed her hair to one side of her face. "Who said you had to wait? I'm ready when you are."

Joe stared at her in awe, as if he'd just discovered the mother lode of sex. "You are amazing, do you know that?"

"Yes. Now, lie still like a good cowboy." In one fluid motion, she pushed herself up to a sitting position, straddling his muscled belly like he was a stallion underneath her, and reached for the box of condoms he'd tossed onto the nightstand. As he watched her, she opened it and pulled out one cellophane-wrapped little prize. Grinning triumphantly, waggling it in her grip, she resettled herself full-length on Joe's chest—as if she were lying atop a surfboard—and tore open the package.

"Are you going to wear it, too?"

She laughed. "Naughty man. If I could, you wouldn't like me."

"True."

With the packaged condom still in her hand, Meg again pushed herself up to sit on Joe's rock-hard belly. This time, though, she scooted down on him— being mindful of certain parts that can only be bent back so far—until she was perched lightly on his thighs. Between them, the evidence of his desire jutted and grew. Meg raised an eyebrow in admiration.

"My, my, cowboy. Lucky for me you're not from Texas…where everything's even bigger."

"Not so fast, ma'am. I was born in Austin, the capital of Texas."

"I'll say. Now, hold still because I've never done this before."

Joe bucked in surprise. "What the hell, Meg? You've never done this before? Are you serious?"

She'd kept her seat by tensing her thighs around his and grabbing for his sides. Mercifully, she hadn't reached for the obvious handhold. "Be still. You nearly knocked me off. I meant I haven't ever put one of these on a guy before." She pulled the condom out of the package and studied the lubricated circle of latex. "So this thing will actually be ribbed when it's unfurled, huh?"

"For the love of— Yes, that's what the box says."

"Well, the box should know. Anyway, by the time I'm through, this guy will be in his little *Saturday Night Fever* suit and hot to trot."

"Well, I can't say I've ever heard it put that way and far be it from me to stop you in all this, Meg, but do you really just want to…get it on? I mean this is our first time. You don't want—"

"Yes, I do want. I want everything. Just not this time. We can go slow and tender the next time, okay? Right now I want rough and ready. Now, hold still."

"I haven't moved."

Again, Meg met Joe's wonderfully blue-eyed and intense gaze. "I wasn't talking to that end of you, specifically."

"I see. Still, you might want to speed things up down there before you, uh, don't have much left to work with."

"Don't worry. I know how to fix that, too."

Joe flopped back on the pillows. "I have died and gone to heaven and you are my reward for—"

The sudden, strident ringing of the phone beside the bed cut off Joe's sentiment. Meg cried out in surprise, losing her grip on the condom and snapping it against his most sensitive part—which caused Joe to curse, and ended with Meg also cursing as she relaxed back on his legs. She pointed to his withering manhood. "Oh, now look what's happened. Damn it all to hell, I finally get you in bed—and then this." She indicated with an angry, sweeping gesture the bedside phone with its red blinking light. "Every time you touch me or kiss me, the freakin' phone rings."

The ringing continued. Joe divided his attention between Meg and the telephone. "It could be Uncle Maury. I couldn't reach him earlier, even though I called about twenty times. Or Linda, if she's called him and forced him to tell her where I am."

"I guess you have to answer it. At this time of night, something could be wrong," she said, defeat ringing in her voice as she dismounted Joe's thighs, flopped over onto the bed and pulled the top sheet over her.

"I hope it's Maury," Joe said, finally reaching for the handset. "Because if it's Linda, we might not be able to get Mr. *Saturday Night Fever* on the dance floor again tonight."

10

IT WAS LINDA. And it wasn't pleasant. Not for her, and not for Joe. Ten minutes into the conversation, with him naked and sitting on the side of the king-size bed with Meg, his back to her, Joe ran a hand through his hair and blew out a breath. "Look, I'm sorry you had to find out this way. It wasn't something I planned or could have foreseen…. What?… No, I did not haul ass for a cheap beach motel with the first willing chick I came across. Come on, Linda, it's not like you to say something like that. Besides, where I am right now is about the farthest thing from a motel you could ever—"

He listened to her strained, tense voice telling him that the number of stars the hotel might have earned from the travel guides was not the point. "I agree. I was just trying to get that image out of your head. Look, the truth is, there's a situation here with Uncle Maury—I know you talked to him and I know he sounded fine, but he isn't." On one level, Joe was thrilled Linda had reached the old guy. Where the hell could he have been all evening? "Look, he might even be delusional right now…. Oh, come on, just listen to me a minute—"

He pulled the receiver from his ear and stared at it.

"Did she hang up on you again?" Meg said drowsily from behind him, the swishing of the sheets telling him she was shifting position.

"You could say that," Joe said, putting down the phone. "Well, at least we know Uncle Maury's all right."

"I heard you say that about her talking to him. That's good."

"Yeah." Joe still stared at the phone, feeling both guilty and relieved.

"Joe?" Meg softly asked. "Are you all right? You want to talk? I'm a good listener."

That made the decision easy, didn't it? Joe replaced the handset in its cradle. *Goodbye, Linda.* He pivoted to see Meg…and froze. Damn, she was something. Despite the myriad emotions he was feeling right now, he was after all still a man who could not help but notice how sexy Meg was without even trying. She just oozed an earthy sensuality, with her lightly tanned skin and dark hair and eyes. A total seductress…naked in his bed…and so far, nothing had happened. Actually, he didn't see how it could, either, after Linda's mood-shattering phone call.

Meg shrugged the sheet down far enough to get her left arm out from under the covers, and her movement left the soft mound of her breast only barely covered. Joe swallowed, not feeling the least bit guilty anymore. Just turned on. After all, there was nothing he could do about Linda—it had ended badly. He'd hoped it wouldn't have to, but it had. Maybe it was cleaner this way. Maybe… He couldn't take his eyes off Meg. He'd thought she was going to stretch like a cat, but instead she held her hand out to him.

"Give me the phone. I want to call Carl. It's only fair we both get hung up on in the same night by former lovers, don't you think?"

Joe chuckled, surprising himself that he could. He passed her the phone's handset. "And just where are you going to call him? Here or at his place?"

"Both, if I have to. Maybe on his cell phone."

"You'll blow your cover."

"I don't care anymore. I just want this dealt with and over. So, what do I dial for room-to-room calls?"

Joe studied the phone's cradle with all its instructions. "Uh…eight and then the room number. Which we don't know. Hell. Call the front desk and ask them to connect you to his room. Easy enough."

Meg nodded, pushed zero and put the receiver to her ear. She smiled at Joe. He winked at her. Without looking away from him, she spoke into the phone. "Yes, good evening. Could you connect me, please, to Mr. Carl Woodruff's room?… Thank you." Cool as an ice cube, she waited, blatantly running her gaze up and down Joe. "Hey, cowboy, what happened to your little rubbery buddy— Yes, hello…. I'm sorry, what?" Talking to whomever was at the other end of the line, she grinned triumphantly at Joe. "I see. Mr. and Mrs. Woodruff checked out? Really? How long ago?… Thirty minutes ago? Well, I can't imagine what must have happened. Thank you."

As soon as she hung up, she curled up in a delicious little ball of naughtiness under the sheet, clamped a hand over her grinning mouth and laughed. "Oops. Trouble in paradise. We are so bad."

Feeling smug, Joe took the handset from her and

hung it up. "No more than he deserved, the jerk. You want to try his cell phone?"

"Sure. He wouldn't have had time to get home yet." A perfectly wicked light suddenly shone from Meg's eyes. "So I wonder if that means—"

"Gotcha. *Mrs. Woodruff* is still in the car with him—assuming she rode over here with him, right?"

"Right. Ten bucks says she did." Meg abruptly sat up, apparently forgetting her state of undress as the sheet fell away from her and pooled in her lap.

Joe stared at her.

"Joe? What's wrong—" She followed his enraptured gaze to her chest, gasped and tugged the sheet up to hold it modestly over her bare breasts. "Shame on you, sir."

Joe inhaled sharply as if he'd just been given a much-needed hit of oxygen from a scuba tank, shook his head and came to himself. "You have very nice breasts, ma'am."

"Yeah?" She tugged the sheet out—but not enough for him to be able to feast his eyes on her again—and stared down at herself. "Hey, they are kind of nice, aren't they?"

"No doubt about it."

He watched her dial. "Go get 'im, tiger."

"Thanks. I do wish I could be nicer, but he really doesn't deserve— Hello, Carl, it's Meg. Where are you?… On your way home? From where?… Oh, a family wedding. How nice. Where was it? Yes, that is a nice hotel. Very romantic. So, who got married? Your niece?" Meg put her hand over the speaker part of the handset and whispered fiercely to Joe. "The lunkhead! He can't have a niece. He doesn't have any brothers or sisters. What a crock of— What? No, I'm not talking to someone. I thought you were. Did you go alone to the wedding? You did?" Meg rolled her eyes. "Well, that couldn't have been any fun. So, listen, I won't keep you. I just called to tell you I thought about your proposal and, I'm sorry, but I have to say no. It was nice of you to ask, but I don't think your current Mrs. Woodruff there in the car with you— Hello?"

Meg held the receiver out and stared at it. She raised her mock-concerned gaze to meet Joe's thoroughly amused one. "I think we got cut off."

Joe took the phone from her and hung it up. "Imagine that. Come here, you sweet little naked thing, you. Nothing's going to stop us this time."

AND NOTHING DID. Joe could not believe he finally got to hold this delicious woman in his arms and breathe in the perfume at the nape of her graceful neck. The way it mingled with the flowery scent of her skin made him wild. If only the very air could smell like her. Lying atop her, kissing her, feeling her arms around his neck, her breasts pressed against his chest, her soft mound against his hardness, it took everything Joe had to hold back long enough to get to know her body.

Already she was urging him downward on her. Joe obliged, but only as far as her firmly rounded breasts with their deep-rose nipples, already hardened by desire to tight buds. Joe softly took one in his mouth, sucking and nipping and flicking it with his tongue. His reward was Meg arching her back and entangling her hands in his hair. Her breathing quickened until she was panting and saying his name. Her response only inflamed his. Giving up one breast, he kissed his way over to the other, offering it the same indulgent treatment...laving soft circles, with his tongue, around its peak—

"Joe!" Meg bucked under him and arched her back. "Oh my God, you're killing me. I'll pass out—"

"Don't do that. I wouldn't want you to miss this." Showing no mercy, Joe encased her ribs in his hands and languidly kissed his way down her, tasting the sweet wine of the taut skin over her ribs, her concave belly, her navel and down, down to the dark, crisp triangle at the apex of her thighs. "Oh God, Meg, you are beautiful," he said, staring his fill at her goddess's body. "I have to taste you."

"Joe," she moaned.

"I know, baby." Joe dipped his head down and, using his tongue, swirled and separated the protective nest of hair until he found the very center of her. He pressed the tip of his tongue against the tiny bud, holding his place there until she throbbed against him. At that simple touch, Meg made a helpless, gasping noise at the back of her throat that engorged Joe's own desire to an almost painful fullness.

Under him, Meg spread her legs, opening herself to him. Such a sweet, trusting vulnerability she offered him. Moved beyond words, Joe nevertheless feared he would burst with wanting her. Holding her hips gently but firmly in his hands, Joe pulled Meg to him, all but burying his face in her heat. Reveling in the rich, musky smell of her, his own senses on fire with need, Joe forced a discipline on himself that his masculine brain and body bucked hard against. But he held firm, wanting this to be good for Meg, too.

His touch on her most sensitive of places was alternately gentle then demanding, invasive then yielding…until her muscles tightened, her breathing changed and her womanhood began opening to him. She was close. So very close. Joe concentrated his efforts on the tight bud itself, feeling it grow, hearing Meg's fingernails raking up fistfuls of the sheet…. Then she cried out as the rhythmic undulations seized her and convulsed her abdominal muscles.

Burning with desire, Joe rode the wave of her satiation as long as he dared, as long as she would allow. When she moved away from him, begging, "No more, no more, oh God, no more," Joe pulled himself up and held her in his arms, kissing her jaw, her neck, her ear. She again bumped her hips against him.

"Take me, Joe. I need you so badly."

"I need you, too, Meg. God, you don't know how much I need you."

"Then…hurry, cowboy."

Joe raised his head from her neck. "I'm not really a cowboy, you know."

Her eyes popped open. "Is this my fantasy or yours?"

"Ah. Point taken, ma'am. In that case, you're a dance-hall girl."

"Whatever, Joe."

Done torturing her and himself, Joe placed a pecking kiss on her nose and, with quick practiced movements, rolled off her, applied a condom and rolled back to her. Her knees bent and parted, she held her arms out to him in clear invitation, one Joe accepted.

He moved up and over her, slowly lowering himself onto her pelvis. She clutched at his shoulders, her eyes half closed, her lips parted.

Almost of its own accord, Joe's sex pushed against her, seeking entry into her warm and willing body. Holding himself up on his elbows, watching her face, drinking in her delicate features, loving how she wantonly tossed her head from side to side, Joe entered her, sliding in smoothly, filling her.

A great shudder seized his body and it took all he had not to succumb right there. She was so hot and tight. And then…she lifted her hips, taking him more fully inside her. Her body tensed around his shaft and sexual urgency exploded in Joe's body, whipping his very blood into foam. Beyond thought, reason and finesse, he pumped his hips in long and steady strokes that had them both making the unmistakable noises of passion being consummated. Meg wrapped her legs around his hips. Joe responded by pounding into her, knowing instinctually that he wasn't hurting her, even though her fingernails raked his back and she groaned deliciously.

And then…it was there. The moment. The heightened tension. The increased sensitivity…and the peak instant when Joe thrust one last time and held himself rigid over Meg. She took over the thrusting motion with her hips and brought them both to a shouting crescendo of release so hot that it threatened to set off the fire alarm mounted in the ceiling.

With one last, weak motion, Joe collapsed atop Meg, burying his face in the crook of her neck. They were both so slick with lovemaking's sheen that he figured he'd slide right off her and onto the floor, where he would stay until he passed out or died. But Meg had her arms up under his and wrapped around his back, as if holding on to him for dear life. That was good enough for him. Joe laid there, one big charred hunk of love.

About a millennium later, when he was certain he would live, not that he much cared either way right now, Joe raised himself and smiled down into Meg's beautiful face with her dark eyes, pert nose and expressive mouth. She'd never been more beautiful to him than she was at this moment.

A wave of sweet tenderness and fierce protectiveness unexpectedly seized Joe, giving him that feeling that told him this woman was the one who could toss his heart right over a high cliff in gale force winds... and make him love it. *Son of a gun.* He'd met his match. A willing victim, Joe chuckled as he gently pushed back dampened tendrils of Meg's long dark hair from her very pink cheeks.

"What's so funny, cowboy?"

"Nothing. All I have to say is...damn, woman."

Sighing, Meg nodded, tipping her tongue out to wet her lips. "I'll say. You're pretty good at this, too."

"Thanks. I was trying out some of my new stuff."

Meg bumped a shoulder against him. "So, you want to do it again?"

"Yes, until I'm a hundred and seventy-four years old. But I'd settle for all night tonight."

Meg rolled her eyes. "Braggart."

"Not me. But I do have a certain reputation to maintain."

"I see. Well, I have one thing to say about that."

"An endorsement?"

"No. You're on my hair, stud."

"Oh, hell, sorry." Joe shifted enough to disengage his body from hers and pull himself off her. "Excuse me a minute, okay?" With that, he rolled to the side of the bed, got up and padded naked around the king-size bed to the bathroom to divest himself of the condom. After washing up, he came back into the bedroom.

"You sure do have a nice butt, Joe."

He stopped short, pivoting so he could see her. Covered by the sheet, Meg lay propped up on her side, her knees bent, her head supported by a hand. Her elbow rested against the mattress. But it was her dark eyes, bright with mischief and boldness, that captured his attention.

"Are you always this forward, lady?"

"Yes. You ought to see me in art museums checking out the ancient statues of naked gods and kings and Greek wrestlers. Have you ever noticed how it's never their package that's gotten lopped off somehow over the centuries? Just their noses or arms or even their whole heads, but not that particular part?"

"Ouch. But no, I can't say I have. And, by the way, have you ever been thrown out of any museums for unseemly behavior?"

Meg shrugged. "Once or twice. Hey, I can't help it if I was curious."

"Yeah, I bet you were. Are you still?"

She rolled over onto her back and held her arms out to him. "Come here and I'll show you…"

THE NEXT AFTERNOON as they headed back to Tampa in The Stogie, Meg reflected that they hadn't done it until Joe was a hundred and seventy-four, but they had done it all morning, until dangerously close to check-out time. All in all, a good compromise. Sitting next to him now, her hand resting on his bare thigh below the hem of his khaki shorts, she smiled dreamily as she reveled in the achy soreness of her muscles and the swollen throbbiness of a certain other place.

"Man, those guys just don't give up. They're still back there," Joe said, breaking into Meg's reverie.

It took her a moment…."Oh. Our official escort, you mean?"

"Yep. In a big black stretch limo. They're about as subtle as a sledgehammer for people who've been on our tail since the hotel. Like we wouldn't spot them."

"I don't think they care if we do." Meg smiled and suppressed the impulse to glance over her shoulder. "But is it really them, Joe? They could just be innocent rich people or newlyweds in a rented limo."

"Could be. But the driver, from what I can see in the rearview mirror, is a big muscled guy dressed in black."

"Really? Can you see if it's one of the guys I ran into by the elevators?"

"It might be. He's staying too far back for me to tell."

"You know what? I am so over them. I don't even care who they are. Pull over to the shoulder, Joe. If they stop behind us, then we'll have our answer—"

"And then what?"

"And then I'm going to get out and give them a piece of my mind and pepper spray them like I should have done last night."

"There's a good plan."

"Well, you think of something, then. You're the

one who brought them up. I was sitting here happily thinking about…" She'd barely caught herself before revealing her innermost thoughts and had to finish lamely with "…stuff."

But it wasn't lost on him. Joe nudged her with his shoulder. "Stuff, huh?"

Meg pinched his thigh. "Turn the page, Joe."

Though he laughed at her teasingly, he heeded her warning. "Okay, forget the car behind us. New topic."

"Like what?"

"Like all these exotic flowers and the jungle vegetation and big, leafy palm trees everywhere." His window was rolled down so he could rest an elbow there. Earlier he'd told her he wanted to work on his trucker's tan. "Complete culture shock, you know, coming from Denver. Makes me feel…"

He'd paused, frowning as if searching for a word, one Meg was happy to supply.

"Tropical? Like you might want to wear a grass skirt and a coconut bra?"

He grinned over at her. "Well, I would, but the big kids on the playground would tease me. However, I would like to see *you* dressed like that."

Ever cooperative, Meg shrugged her willingness. "Okay, but you'd have to wear a Stetson and chaps for me. And nothing else. Well, except for cowboy boots." She pictured that little vision in her mind's eye—and started adding to it. "And spurs. Oh, and a gun. A big, shiny six-shooter strapped to your hip in a holster. And maybe—"

"And maybe try out for the Village People? All I said was I like your palm trees, and the next thing I know, I'm suited up for a pornographic cattle drive."

Meg chuckled. "So, I take it there aren't a lot of those in Denver? Palm trees, I mean."

"No, I'd say there are about as many palm trees in Denver as there are inches of snow in Florida." Joe breathed in deeply, contentedly. "Man, smell that air. I never knew before that you could actually smell sunshine and warmth. Wow. I am really going to miss all this."

Miss all this? Meg froze in place, despite the warm air billowing through the car's interior. "What do you mean—" she had to stop and swallow hard "—you'll miss it?"

Joe glanced over at her. "Are you all right? What's wrong?"

She sighed. "Where are you going, Joe?"

Joe frowned his obvious confusion. "We're going back to Uncle Maury's, remember?"

Meg shook her head. "Not that. The bigger picture. Are you going back to Denver? Is that what you mean?"

He looked at her as if he'd never seen her before. "Well, yeah. Of course I am. I live there. But we still have a week before—"

"Stop this car, Joe Rossi."

"What?"

"You heard me. Stop this car." Anger and betrayal wormed their way into Meg's heart. She scooted across the seat, as far away from him as she could get, until her shoulder was pressed against the passenger door. She fought her seat belt. At last she had it undone and—

"What'd I say? What's wrong, Meg?" Joe reached out for her, but Meg batted his hand away. Looking thoroughly confused, he returned his hand to the steering wheel. "Okay, I'm not even going to pretend I know what's going on."

"Oh…ha! You know exactly what's going on, mister. And if you don't, you should. And I said stop this car right now."

Joe glanced from the road to her. "Where, exactly? We're in three lanes of traffic and about to get on a long bridge. Just tell me what's wrong or what I did."

Meg poked out her bottom lip. "How can you not know what's wrong? You just breeze into my life, whisk me away from my home, break up my romance—"

"Break up your romance?" Joe looked at her as if she'd just sprouted horns. "Oh, please. You broke up with Carl a week before you ever met me."

"All right, fine, but then you take me to hotels and weddings and make mad, passionate love to me— and now you're just going to abandon me and go home? Just like that?"

Apparent enlightenment dawned. "Oh, honey, is that why you're upset? Come on, Meg…no, it's not like that at all."

His obvious striving for a reasonable tone only further irritated her.

"I live in Denver. My job is there. My family's there. It's not easy to simply—"

"What about Maury? He's your family, and he's here. And there're lots of construction jobs here, too. Year-round."

"All that's true. But…hell, Meg, I don't know what you want me to do. I love Denver. The mountains, the snow, the cold. The wild West is all I've ever known.

And you and I are still so new with each other that we haven't even—"

"Don't you dare say you have to think about us, Joe Rossi, because we both know what that means." Meg looked up and away, determined, by sheer will, that the tears blurring her vision would not fall. When they did, anyway, she turned away from Joe, staring out the window to her right as she miserably wiped them away.

"Meg? Are you crying?" He sounded surprised, even upset.

"No," she said, a sob catching in her voice and giving her away.

"Oh, man," he drawled, sounding sick about it, "now I've made you cry."

The Stogie suddenly jerked to the right, forcing Meg to grab for the door. Startled, her tears instantly dried, she looked to Joe, whose eyebrows were lowered dangerously. "What are you doing? Where—"

"I'm doing exactly what you said earlier. I'm pulling over. And this time you're going to listen to me—for once."

11

As it turned out, Joe's timing for reaching the end of his emotional rope was impeccable. Because at hand was an easy exit off the highway, which he took—none too smoothly—onto an unpaved, sandy road that ran the length of a long, narrow strip of beach that ended where the bridge ahead began. Dotting the sand, along the gleaming water's edge, were tall, leafy, protective stands—clumps, really—of mangroves.

Every natural break between the water-loving plants boasted a car, minivan or truck parked in it. Not surprisingly, then, the area teemed with swimmers, sunbathers, picnickers, boaters, daredevils on Jet Skis, and families with pets and kids. A Sno-Kone truck, a hot-dog vendor and a guy renting Jet Skis completed the picture. All right, so it wasn't the best place for a private conversation, but too bad. This was where it was going to happen.

The Stogie, being what it was—a magnet for old-car enthusiasts—already had the attention of about half the men on the beach. Only too aware of his audience, Joe brought his ride to a stop alongside the hard-packed sandy track. He was embarrassed to admit, even to himself, that they looked more like the

Clampetts pulling up in front of their Beverly Hills mansion than some race-car driver coolly pulling his purebred machine into the pit for service.

Still, several men whooped and hollered, raising their plastic cups high in salute. Totally self-conscious, Joe cut the engine and waved across Meg to what he hoped were his admirers. Only then did he register the uncertainty stamped on her expression. He sat back.

"What's wrong?"

"Nothing against all these nice people here, Joe, and I'm really not a snob, but, well…there's a reason the cops are always patrolling this little strip of beach."

"I can believe that." Again, he looked around her, considering the beachgoers ranged up and down the sandy spit of land to their right. As far as he could see, they'd pretty much returned to their business. Or pleasure, he supposed. "But they're not bothering us, and since we didn't come here to join them for a wienie roast and a day of drinking, we should be okay. But if it gets ugly, there's always your pepper spray, right?"

Joe had sought to reassure her a bit, but Meg had no smile for him. Instead, she sat there facing forward, her lips pinched together. The very image of a woman not reassured. *Well, great.* Not knowing whether to be mad, concerned or amused—maybe all three—Joe ran his gaze over her. Dressed in shorts and a halter top, her dark hair up in a windblown ponytail that left baby curls framing her temple and the nape of her neck, she looked about fourteen years old.

Joe had to swallow back a chuckle that threatened.

No doubt, she'd take it wrong, maybe think he was laughing at her, when the truth was, he would be laughing at himself. Why? Because Meg Kendall turned him and his emotions every which way but loose. He wanted to shout his joy and his frustration with her. Just grab her up, hug her tight and kiss her all over. She was so damned cute and exasperating. She did the strangest things to his heart, like make him want to fight the whole world to keep her safe. Or do stupid tricks to win her love.

"Okay, so we're here," she said abruptly, still staring out through the windshield. "What am I supposed to be listening to *for once,* as you put it?"

He stared at her unyielding profile. "I can't figure this out, Meg. Why are we at each other's throats?"

She turned her head to look at him. "That was rhetorical, right, since the answer is so obvious?"

Joe hated it when women said that, because it was never obvious to him. Never. "Rhetorical. Okay, sure, why not?"

"And that was, too?"

Shooting her a ha-ha look, he sat back against the seat and pushed his fingers through his hair, too late realizing that with the wind from the rolled-down car windows, it must already be standing on end. *I probably look like Stan Laurel right now.* And why not? This was certainly another fine mess he'd got himself into. Trying again, Joe glanced Meg's way.

"So, you want to get out and talk?"

"Unless you have dueling weapons with you, and then I'd rather do that."

Her continued sarcasm spiked Joe's temper. "Really? Well, we might be in luck. From the looks of some of those good ol' boys over there lurking around that big gnarly pickup truck, I'd say more than one of them could come up with some illegal weapons we could use, if you want me to go ask."

She shrugged. "Go ahead. But maybe you should take my pepper spray in case they get rough with you." Her chin in the air, like that of some snooty poodle, she got out of the car and slammed the door closed behind her.

Insulted, Joe called out to her through the open window, "Hey, you, I can take care of myself. I do work in construction, in case you forgot. But, thanks, my masculine pride is still firmly intact."

"Who cares?" She leaned her butt against the rear passenger door and crossed her arms.

"I care." Not about to be the one sitting and sulking in the car, Joe got out, only to have his senses immediately assaulted by the relentless sunlight beating down on his head, the mocking cry of seagulls and the scent of the salt-tangy air. Ticked off, he pivoted to his left, intending to circle around behind the back of the antique vehicle and go have it out, once and for all, with Meg. But the sight that greeted him stopped him in midstride.

About twenty or thirty yards back from where Joe had brought The Stogie to a halt, the big black stretch limo sat idling. Somehow, he hadn't given their tail another thought once he'd pulled off the highway. He supposed he'd figured it would just continue on. *Wrong.* The car seemed to crouch menacingly low to the ground, like a wildcat bunching its muscles to spring on a promising meal. If there was any good news here, it was that the big guys inside hadn't gotten out...yet.

"Oh, man, just what I need," Joe muttered.

He walked around to where Meg still stood in the same pose, hips leaned against the car door, arms crossed. She spared Joe a glance as he stopped in front of her, putting his hands in his shorts pockets. Just to gauge her mood, he said, "We have company."

"You mean them?" She sent a wave in the direction of the limo.

"Hey, let's not invite them over."

"I was just greeting them—not that they waved back. How rude. But what's the problem, Joe? You don't think they're anybody but Maury's friends."

He shrugged. "I could be wrong."

"Are you serious?" Her voice said he better not be. "Now—after everything we've been through with these guys—now you think they're Mafia?"

"Maybe. Don't look at me like that. Women aren't the only ones who can change their minds. But I'll tell you this, those hulks get out of that car and I'm calling the cops. They can't just openly follow us, like they've been doing, and then pull off the road like that right behind us."

"Yes, they can, Joe. This *is* a public beach."

"You know what I mean. These guys aren't here for the tropical weather. They're stalking us and—I don't give a damn who they are—that's a threat."

"Really? You feel threatened? I don't. I think they could just be nice concerned guys—"

"Oh, stop right there. Are you telling me that now you don't think they're the Mafia? Is that it?" He shook his head. "Unbelievable."

After two days of hysterics over these same guys, Meg now shrugged like it was no big deal. "No, it isn't. I think they like me and—"

"Have appointed themselves your personal body-guards who intend to follow you everywhere you go for the rest of your life? Well, I'm not okay with that. I don't think you're safe around them."

"Maybe they don't think I'm safe around you."

That hurt. "Do *you* think you're safe around me, Meg?"

Instantly apologetic, as if she realized she'd gone too far, she abandoned her standoffish attitude. She put her hand on his forearm and sighed, resigned. "Of course I think I'm safe with you. I know I am. I'm sorry." She paused, then added. "Actually, I'm over those guys following us, too. I wish they'd go away."

With his ruffled feathers settled, Joe said, "I agree. But forget about them for a minute. They don't have anything to do with what's going on between us."

"No, they don't. You're right." Withdrawing her hand from his arm, Meg retreated to her original po-sition against the car. And there she waited, watch-ing his face.

Joe was quiet for a moment, gathering his thoughts. Then he said, softly, "So, Meg, what's going on here? I mean, between you and me. Why were you crying?"

She lowered her gaze and pushed the toe of her sandal through the sand. "Because I want you to stay here with me," she told her feet. "Or I did. Now I'm not so sure."

"You've gone from *sure* to *not so sure* in the amount of time it took me to pull off the highway?" With her head still lowered, she nodded. His heart melting, Joe stared at the top of her head, noting the brilliant highlights in her dark auburn hair, almost gold, and wondering why this had to be so hard. "Meg, can you look at me, please?" He waited until she did. Her big, brown eyes sparkled with reflected sunlight...or more tears—he couldn't tell which. "Why aren't you sure now?"

She shrugged. "I don't know. Maybe because it's not the same if I have to tell you, or ask you, or beg you to stay. I can't believe you're leaving me just like that." She snapped her fingers for emphasis.

"I'm not leaving you 'just like that.' Go with me back to Denver."

Although Meg's surprised gaze locked with his, Joe felt certain she could not be more shocked than he was that he'd just extended an invitation to her to join him in his life. Did he mean it? Did he really want that? What if she accepted? What would he do if she did—or if she didn't? This was major. How could he have said something so—

"No," Meg said, her voice actually sounding dismissive. "I can't go to Linda-land. I live here, and my family and friends are here. So is my job, and school's not even out for another two months. You're sweet to ask, but you have to be reasonable about this, Joe."

"*I* have to be reasonable?" Joe felt stunned. Then he was all outrage and broad gestures. "What, are you kidding me here? I had to pull off the road—" he pointed to it "—not ten minutes ago because you—" he pointed at her "—were crying over my saying I had to go home to my job and family. Then I—" he pointed at himself "—ask you to come to

Denver with me, and you say you can't for the very same reasons I gave for not staying here?"

"Yes."

"Yes? That's it? That's all you have to say? It's okay when those are your reasons, but not when they're mine? What the hell is reasonable about that, Meg?"

She pulled away from the car and got in his face. "Everything. I'm not the one leaving me and Florida, Joe. You are."

He threw his arms out at his sides and shook his head. "Hell, yeah, I'm leaving Florida. I have to. I don't live here."

"Oh, come on, it's not like your visa is expiring. You live in Colorado, not some foreign place."

"What if the situation were reversed and you'd come to Denver and I wanted you to stay there? What would you do?" he asked.

"Well, of course, I'd have to think about it—"

"A-ha!" Joe pointed accusingly at her. "We know what that means, don't we. So *you* would need time to think, but *I'm* not allowed—"

The intrusive sounds of opening and closing car doors cut Joe off. At the same time as Meg, he turned to look in the direction of the Mafia-mobile. Sure enough, the big guys—the ones from the elevator last night—had got out and were now standing beside the car. Despite their dark sunglasses, they were making no secret of the fact that they were watching them.

"Uh-oh, Joe," Meg said fatalistically, drawing his attention to her, where he saw she'd bracketed her waist with her hands, "now you've done it."

Disbelief pinched his features. "Now *I've* done it? I didn't do anything." That sounded lame, even to him. "You know what? This is a bunch of bull. Are you as tired of those yokels interrupting us as I am?" With that, Joe stalked off toward the limo.

"Is that another rhetorical question?" she called after him.

"Yes," he yelled back. Within seconds, Joe sensed, rather than saw or heard, Meg on his heels. Who was surprised? But he had bigger problems in front of him, meaning the closer he got to his quarry, the larger the men loomed. Undaunted—or, at least telling himself he was—Joe stopped in front of the man named Rocco.

"All right, look, just who the hell are you guys, anyway? What do you want?"

The two wingmen raised their eyebrows above the rims of their sunglasses. But Rocco showed no response. In fact, he ignored Joe, choosing instead to speak to Meg, who'd stopped beside Joe.

"You okay? Is he *embarrassing* you again?"

"No. We were just talking."

Joe felt vindicated...but too soon, because Meg added, "He's going to leave me and go back to Denver."

Rocco raised his sunglasses off his nose and stared at Joe, who saw narrowed eyes as deeply black as onyx marbles.

"Is that true?"

Since, by all appearances, he was about to be stomped into a mud hole, Joe figured he might as well make his last words memorable. "Is it any of your business?"

Resettling his shades, the man surprised Joe by chuckling, apparently in admiration. "You got guts,

I'll give you that. So, why are you leaving this fine lady? You nuts or something? Look at her."

Automatically, Joe did as this unlikely relationship counselor suggested. He looked at Meg, who returned his gaze from apprehension-rounded eyes. Incredibly cute, she was. And brave and stubborn. And intelligent and kind and funny and sexy... among her many other fine attributes. Suddenly, Joe knew what he was going to do. "I wasn't leaving her. Not forever. I was coming back."

"You were?" Meg said in unison with her defender. Joe watched her exchange a glance with Rocco.

"I didn't know that part yet," she told him, grinning.

Joe caught the cheery looks on the faces of the two backup singers, or shooters—whatever—who flanked the talkative one of their trio.

"So how come you didn't tell her you meant to come back?" Rocco said, recapturing Joe's attention. "No reason to upset the lady."

"I never meant to upset the lady." He hoped his terse reply served notice that he had no intention of further discussing his love life with a helpful godfather, or whoever the hell he was.

"I see." The man was nodding, causing the sunlight to bounce off his slicked-back hair. "So, are we good here?" he asked, checking his wristwatch. "We still have business to conduct today in Tampa, so if there are no questions—"

"I have a question," Meg said.

Her defender smiled benevolently. "Ask away, sweetheart."

"Thanks. How'd you know my name? I never told it to you last night, but you called me Meg."

"Ah, that. Let's just say…I do my homework." He turned to Joe. "Are we done here?"

Joe nodded.

"Good." With a flick of his jacket, the man turned away. His two henchmen jumped into action, one opening a door and standing back, the other sprinting around to the driver's side.

Right before he got into the back seat of the stretched vehicle, Rocco turned again to Joe. "You're a cute couple. You should kiss and make up. But, just so you know, once we all get to Maury's, I'd stay out of the way if you don't want to get hurt."

Less than thirty minutes later, with a disgruntled Meg stationed at the big picture window in his uncle's living room, where Joe had posted her as designated watch for the bad guys, he stood in Maury's bedroom and watched the frenzy of packing the little old guy was engaged in.

Maury was yanking open drawers, sorting through them, tossing a hodgepodge of mismatched clothes toward his bed, where he'd placed an old-fashioned, beat-up suitcase that looked to be every bit as ancient as its owner. About every third toss of loud pants and gaudy shirts actually hit the suitcase. Everything else hit the carpeted floor or adorned the ceiling fan's blades. Luckily, it wasn't turned on.

All of this would have been comical, Joe decided, had the range of possible explanations behind his great-uncle's actions not been so scary. But the very fact that Maury Seeger was packing, after hearing Joe's and Meg's recounting of their last twenty-four hours' worth of close encounters of the mob kind, confirmed for Joe that the events of this weekend had not been orchestrated by Maury as some elaborate game. They were serious. However, the question remained, what exactly was going on?

Joe knew he ought to call the police. But he was stopped by two things. One, the bad guys weren't anywhere around, so he could hardly call and ask the police to stake out the place just in case some threat materialized. Not that he looked forward to telling his tale to the cops, who would most likely haul him off as a nutcase.

And two, Joe didn't know yet the extent of his great-uncle's involvement in all this. Bottom line? What if he called the law and it turned out that Uncle Maury was among those taken to jail? He might deserve it, but Joe didn't think he could live with knowing he'd sent the old man up. Especially when his family found out. He'd rather have the Mafia on his back than his mother.

Joe's only hope, then, was to get quickly to the truth and hope he had enough intellect and cunning to devise a plan that would *not* get them killed but *would* make this go away. As if that wasn't enough, he needed to accomplish everything in the unknown amount of time he had between right now and the moment the trouble came knocking—which could be in the next second. Hence, he was forced to bully a beloved old man more than fifty years his senior.

"All right, Uncle Maury," Joe said, "we've told you everything—" well, not about the sex "—that's happened with us. Now it's your turn. No more games because I'm thinking those limousine lizards could show up at any minute. And when they do, it won't be for tea and cookies."

Standing in front of his chest of drawers and checking out a blaringly loud Hawaiian shirt he had wadded up in his hands, Maury smelled the garment, grimaced and tossed it to the floor. "Relax, Joey. Don't worry about it. Those guys don't scare me."

"Right." Joe crossed his arms over his chest.

His back to Joe, Maury next held up a lime-green knit pullover, which he was studying. "I'm serious. They don't. They wouldn't make pimples on the butts of real hit men."

"Imagine my relief…when I'm dead."

Maury turned to him, looking stern. "Don't get smart with me, Joey. I can still turn you over my knee."

Joe let that one slide. "So, all right, these guys don't scare you. Why are you packing?"

"What? This?" He pointed to the suitcase on his bed. "This ain't got nothin' to do with them."

Joe's bark of laughter was humorless. "Again… right."

"I ain't lying. Here, smell this shirt. Tell me what you think." He advanced on Joe, the shirt held out in front of him.

Joe pulled back. "I don't think so. Just put it in the suitcase."

"Good enough for me." Maury did an about-face, heading for his bed, but only making a circuit as he tossed the shirt in the suitcase and made for the nightstand, where he bent over and tugged on the bottom drawer. When he finally yanked it open, several balled-up pairs of black socks—the only color he seemed to own—sprang for freedom from the over-stuffed space and landed around Maury's feet. "Son of a bitch," he muttered, bending over to retrieve them. "One of these days I got to clean out this drawer. I can't find nothin' in here."

Joe watched all this, his heart softening. The old guy was as sweet and good as he was frustrating and hardheaded. Though he hated like hell badgering his uncle, Joe knew he had no choice. Only too aware of the ticking clock hanging over all their heads, he made another effort.

"So, Uncle Maury, when you saw these guys Friday night, what'd you talk about?"

Standing over his suitcase with about half a dozen pairs of those black socks in his hands, Maury said, "We didn't talk about nothin'."

And there it was: the last straw. "Then what the hell has this past weekend been about?" Joe demanded. "All the running around and the hiding? Come on, I met the guys. I talked to them. They exist."

"I ain't sayin' they don't exist, and that they ain't after me," Maury said. "They do and they are, I know that, Joey. I ain't senile. All I'm sayin' is, I didn't let 'em in for no chat when they showed up, so we never *talked*. What we did was we yelled our business through the door and made a lot of threats. When I wouldn't open up, they left. I think they was afraid of drawin' too much attention to their sorry selves. But that was when I called you—and the rest you know."

"You think I'd be in here questioning you like this if I knew the rest? The only one here who knows the whole truth, Uncle Maury, is you."

The elderly man eyed him warily. "Yeah? What is it you think I know?"

"Okay, how about this? Where were you until

sometime after midnight last night? Meg and I were worried when we couldn't get you on the phone."

The stocky octogenarian's belligerence bled away, leaving his round little face a bright red, which scared the hell out of Joe until he realized his uncle was blushing, not dying. "What, I got a curfew now, Joey?"

Affection won out over exasperation and had Joe chuckling. "Man, you'd have a leash if I didn't think you could slip it."

Maury favored him with a flash of a smile. "I could do that, you know."

"Like I said." Joe studied the older man, wondering where he could have been last night that would embarrass him. Maybe this line of questioning would prove to be the pulled thread that unraveled the entire messed-up tapestry of the past forty-eight hours. "So, anyway," Joe said conversationally, "Meg and I thought about returning to Tampa last night to look for you. The only thing stopping us was that we had no idea where to start."

Looking as relieved as he did guilty about something, Maury lobbed the socks, one bundle at a time, into his suitcase's rapidly filling interior. "That was real smart of you to stay put, Joey, because it wasn't no big deal. See, what happened was I went to take my heart medicine and saw I only had the one pill left. So I had to go to the pharmacy for a refill. End of story."

"Right." Joe knew from long experience that his uncle used the heart medicine line only when he was angling for a sympathetic reaction that would derail anyone who got too close to a truth Maury didn't want revealed. Joe crossed his arms over his chest.

"And where's this pharmacy—in Tallahassee? I'll bet I called twenty times last night."

"There was a long line."

"How long was it?"

Apparent disbelief had Maury searching Joe's face. "What's the matter with you? You think I had all those sick people number off or something? I don't know how many. A bunch. I think something's going around." He coughed for good measure.

Joe raised a skeptical eyebrow. "Yeah, that has to be it. Well, at least Linda managed to reach you last night."

Maury looked suddenly pained. "Yeah. Look, I'm sorry about that, Joey, but I had to tell her. She wouldn't let up on me. The woman's a barracuda. You're better off without her."

"Well, thank you, Maury, my friend and neighbor. I told him the same thing last night," Meg said, entering the bedroom.

12

"SEE, JOEY?" Maury said. "Even Meggie agrees with me."

Ignoring his uncle and tensing with alarm, Joe turned to Meg. She had been instructed not to leave her post unless she saw the bad guys drive up. And here she was. *Oh, hell.* Joe's pulse immediately began racing. He didn't know where to look first, what he could use as a weapon. "Are they here, Meg? Did you see something?"

"I'll say I did." Walking into the room, totally unconcerned as she affectionately patted his arm on her way past, she headed toward the king-size bed.

This forced Joe to follow her. "Well, Meg? What'd you see? Where are they?"

She turned to him and looked surprised to see him following her so closely. "Calm down, Joe. It was just Mrs. Warden, the property manager, on her daily rounds. No doubt she's looking for young people who think life is fun. We all know that's got to be nipped in the bud."

"Hey, Meggie, leave off." Maury's voice was mildly scolding. "Vera Warden ain't so bad, once you get to know her."

Meg mouthed *yikes* at Joe and sat on the end of Maury's bed. "I'm sorry, Maury. I forgot you like her."

"Meg. About the *mob*..." Blatantly ignored, apparently the only one here concerned for their collective safety, Joe stood there, exasperated.

Meg looked up at him questioningly. "There's no mob around. In fact, nothing is going on outside." She shrugged. "And Larry, Moe and Curly aren't much for chitchat."

"Goldfish never are." Joe glared at her, trying his best to convey, without actually saying it, that if the bad guys weren't at the door, she should be at her post.

"Oh, look at you, General Rossi. May I please have a blindfold and a last cigarette before I'm shot?" When he didn't relent, she rearranged her features into that of the misunderstood heroine and raised her chin. "I'll have you know I came back here for a very good reason, Sergeant Bossy Britches."

Ignoring his demotion in rank, Joe said mildly, "Which you are now going to tell me, right?"

"Right. I realized the bad guys might be sneaky enough to park on the other side of the complex, and I'd never see them until they walked right up to the door. Which would be too late. *Or* they could come around the back way and very quietly cut out the glass around the lock on the patio doors in the dining room and enter through there. If they did that, they could easily grab me before I ever heard them. I didn't think you'd want that."

"So to save me that anguish, you came back here."

"Exactly."

"You know what I think?"

Meg looked up at him through her thick eyelashes. "You're going to tell me, aren't you."

"I am. I think the truth is, you were bored and you just wanted to see what we were doing back here."

"You are so cynical, Joe."

"But I'm right, aren't I?"

She ignored that, turning her attention instead to Maury's overflowing suitcase. "What's all this?"

"Uncle Maury's packing. He's running away."

Meg slumped in on herself, a pose of long-suffering. "I thought we just decided those guys aren't real threats."

"No, *we* didn't. *You* decided they aren't, but now *I* believe they are. And, by all appearances, so does my great-uncle, who should know."

Meg sat up, crossing her arms under her breasts— and drawing Joe's attention there, as always. So it was true. A pack of hungry hyenas could be on their heels, and he'd still notice her breasts. When she spoke again, he mustered the decency to raise his gaze quickly.

"Relax. I'm not getting involved, either. He's the one packing."

"Like you'd let him go off on his own. You know how this is going to work out, Joe, so stop him. Stop him now."

Taking offense, Joe stood up straighter. "What do you think I've been trying to do all this time? Watch this and see how far I get." He turned to his uncle— or to where he'd last been—only to see the old guy was no longer in the room. *Damn it!* He appealed to Meg, who smiled tightly and pointed to the open doorway of the adjacent master bathroom.

"Thank you." Joe pursued Maury as far as the bathroom's threshold. There, he found the elderly man scraping a heap of toiletries off the shelves and into his arms—or into the sink when he missed. "Uncle Maury, do you really believe you can give these guys the slip? I don't know how they found you... Hey, how *did* they find you? You're not in the phone book, and you said they were from New Jersey. So...I'm assuming you weren't pen pals?"

"Nothin' like that. But it don't matter. They got connections, Joey. Maybe they found me on that worldwide spiderweb thing. Anyways, what difference does it make? They found me."

"And that's my point. They found you here, so the odds are, they'll find you wherever you go. Why not stay and face them down?"

The old man snorted an abrupt laugh. "Because of what you just said—'face down.' That's how I'd end up. But, look, since I dragged you and Meggie into this, here's the truth."

At last. Joe tensed, preparing himself to hear the worst.

"See, they want what they want," his uncle said, "and I ain't got what they want. Leastwise, not no more. Or not like they think I do. They won't be happy about that, neither. So, bottom line? I ain't too keen to see 'em."

Joe listened, waiting for enlightenment, only slowly realizing that, apparently, his uncle's highly uninformative speech was done. Joe slowly breathed in and out, trying to contain his temper, all the while watching his uncle pluck from the medicine cabinet shelf a much-squeezed tube of some kind of oint-ment, consider it and finally hold it out to Joe.

"You ever tried this here stuff before?" Joe was very pleased to be able to shake his head no. "Well, don't. It burns. Bad." He set it back on the shelf and then searched Joe's face. "Aw, come on, kid. Cheer up. It's okay. Swear to God, I ain't runnin' from those guys who dogged you all weekend. They don't scare me."

His hands in his pockets, Joe leaned a shoulder against the doorjamb, a casual pose that belied his worry. "Well, they scare me."

"Hey, Joe, I'll protect you, honey," Meg called out from her perch on the bed. "The big, bad men like me, remember?"

Joe half turned in the doorway to reply. "Vividly, my little morsel." Seeing her grin, Joe winked at her, then returned his attention to his uncle. "Okay, Uncle Maury, so you're not running. Fine. Then, what is all this packing about?"

Loaded down with enough deodorant and after-shave to supply an entire professional football team, Maury stopped in front of Joe, apparently wanting by. "Excuse me. I got to put this stuff in my suitcase. And the truth is, I'm going to Las Vegas. So are you and Meggie. My treat."

"We're going to Vegas?" Meg called out excitedly.

"No, we are not," Joe assured her, as he again turned sideways allowing his uncle to pass. Once Maury was no longer between him and Meg, Joe could see her bottom lip rolled out in a stubborn pout.

"You're not the boss of me, Joe. You can stay here all you want, but I'm going with Maury."

Joe heaved the sigh of a martyr. "No one's going

anywhere, Meg." She made a show of ignoring him as she set about pulling out and folding the clothes Maury had tossed willy-nilly into his bag. Like there would be points given for neatness. *Great.* Now he had two of them in denial. And open rebellion. "Anyway," he said to the evasive old man, "what's so important out in Vegas?"

"Most people go for the gambling and the show-girls."

"That's why I'm going," Meg declared. When Joe raised his eyebrows and stared at her, she amended, "Well, the shows, for sure. I want to see Celine Dion. And that guy who sings 'Danke Schoen.'"

"Wayne Newton," Maury supplied as he dumped his toiletries into the suitcase and hurried over to the chest of drawers, where he pulled out a stack of folded underwear and made for the bed again. "What about you, Joey? You going or not? I think you should."

Joe flopped on the bed behind Meg and stretched out full length, his hands over his head. "Sure, why the hell not? I give up."

Meg turned to him and rubbed his belly affectionately. "Oh, honey, relax. Look at you trying to be our big hero and keep us all alive. And you've done a great job. We are all still alive." She grinned. "So far."

"Thanks," Joe said dryly, pleased to feel her touch, and wishing it were a little lower.

Maury interrupted the moment by clapping his hands vigorously. "Okay, Joey, Meggie, come on, get up, enough foolin' around. We ain't got all day." Joe's snort of protest was met with Maury's own. "What? Ain't I been packin' this whole time you been standin' around yappin'?"

Though still lying flat on his back, Joe rolled his head until he could see his uncle. "I find I can't argue with that, Uncle Maury."

"About time." Maury directed his attention to the contents of his suitcase. "Something don't look right here, Meggie. Help me see what it is."

Ever cooperative, she sorted through his bag. Joe wondered if she had any idea what they were searching for.

"Never mind. Now I know. I forgot my medicines."

"Uncanny, Maury. I was getting ready to say that," Meg said.

"That's my girl." Maury scooted back into the bathroom and again made a lot of noise rummaging around in there.

Joe turned on his side and put his arm around Meg's slender hips. She favored him with a quick, welcoming smile before continuing to neaten his crazy uncle's suitcase. Toiletries on one side, clothes on the other. Watching her, Joe said, "So, you really think we're not in any danger?"

"No. But you do, don't you?"

"I do. Something's going on with Uncle Maury, Meg. Someone has him scared. He hadn't mentioned needing to pack or going somewhere for pleasure, or any other reason, until we finished telling him our Mafia tales."

"Still, Joe, just because he hadn't told us about it doesn't mean he didn't have this planned. Don't you get it? This is phase two of his big game—a surprise spring-break trip to Las Vegas. He said as much himself. And the proof of that is those Mafia impersonators haven't shown up here, Joe. And why haven't they? Because they're not supposed to. Their part was over once they scared us back there. Now, doesn't that make sense?"

Yes, damn it, it did. It made complete sense, but Joe was just stubborn enough not to want to reverse himself again…so quickly. "Maybe."

Meg chuckled, holding up a big, wide pair of his uncle's boxers for his inspection. "White with red hearts all over them. I wonder if Maury has a lady friend out in Las Vegas?"

Before Joe could formulate a response, Maury hustled back into the room with two bottles of medication and about twenty pounds of shaving apparatus in his arms, which he dumped into the open suitcase. Meg made a distressed sound, seeing all her work wasted. But when Joe's uncle lifted the hem of the Hawaiian shirt he was wearing, exposing his rounded little belly, and pulled out a huge handgun, which he carelessly tossed into the open suitcase, Meg cried out and jumped away from it.

"Son of a bitch, Uncle Maury!" Joe shot up off the bed, his every muscle locked rigidly into place. "You can't take that thing on an airplane. Or anywhere."

"You're right. Not without extra bullets." The old man patted his shorts pockets, then his shirt pockets, as if he expected to find the ammunition in one of them. Then he looked from Meg to Joe. "What's wrong with you two? Is it the gun? Relax. We ain't goin' on no airplane. We're taking The Stogie. Your bags are still packed, right?"

The surreal quality of it all kicked in and had Joe saying, obediently, "Yes."

"Where are they?"

"In The Stogie's trunk—"

"Good. Where's she parked? In the garage?"

"No. Out front."

"Even better," his uncle said, heading back toward his chest of drawers.

As if belatedly pushed from behind, Joe shot forward and reached around Meg to get the gun from the suitcase. Meg scrabbled backward on the bed, evidently determined to put more distance between her and the gun. He pulled the weapon out of the suitcase, handling it gingerly.

Just then came the sound of the doorbell being rung…and rung and rung. An angry battering on the front door followed, accompanied by muffled shouts Joe couldn't quite make out. But the gist was, they'd better open up right now.

"ROTTEN BASTARD," Maury growled. "He's here already." He scooted into his walk-in closet's confines and disappeared.

Terrified, Meg jumped up from the bed, her palms pressed against her cheeks. Her gaze locked with Joe's. "Oh my God, Joe, it's the Mafia! I knew it! What are we going to do?"

Joe narrowed his eyes. "*We're* not going to do anything, but *I'm* going to do exactly what I should have done the first time they—"

"What are you talking about?" Meg's gaze fell to the gun Joe still held in his hand. "What do you think you're going to do?"

The pounding on the door stopped as suddenly as it had started. In the profound silence that followed, Meg met and held Joe's eyes. "No more pounding on the door isn't necessarily good news, is it?"

"No." Joe looked around the room, listening.

"Do you think they left?" Meg whispered.

"No, but I'm going to make certain they don't."

To Meg's horror, Joe pivoted around to face the open bedroom door and took one step in that direction—

"No!" She launched herself at his back, tackling him as she grabbed him from behind and wrapped her arms around his waist. Joe staggered forward. Holding him tightly around the torso, Meg pressed her cheek against his warm, solid back. "If you think for one minute, Joe Rossi, that you're going to open that door to those men, then you're going to have to drag me along with you and get us both killed."

Joe reached around himself and tried to tug her away, pulling unmercifully on her T-shirt. "Come on, Meg, let go."

"No," she wailed, clinging to him.

"For God's sake, they could come bursting through that door at any minute."

"Who cares?"

"What the hell are you doin', Meggie...Joey? This ain't no time to be playin' around."

Meg had forgotten about Maury, who was just now exiting his closet. Since Joe was facing the door to the hallway and Meg was behind him with her head turned to the left, she could see Maury clearly. Not that this was a good thing. Her heart stuttered and very nearly stopped. In his hands, the elderly man held the biggest shotgun she had ever seen in her life.

"Jesus Christ, Uncle Maury! Where the hell did you get that thing?"

Looking mighty grim and determined, Rambo Maury said, "Outta my closet, Joey, where'd you think? You two kids stay here. This is my trouble."

"Like hell it is," Joe drawled, reminiscent—to Meg's stupidly crazed mind—of John Wayne.

Without warning, he twisted violently, no doubt trying again to dislodge her. But Meg danced with mincing steps right around with him, a full three-sixty, still holding tight.

"Come on, Meg. Seriously. I can't let my eighty-year-old uncle go out there alone—"

A boom-boom-boom of pounding hit the front door again and stopped Joe's struggling. Under her cheek, Meg felt the muscles in his back contract with tension. Then someone tried the doorknob, testing to see if it was locked. Apparently, it was because the room didn't fill suddenly with hit men and ricocheting bullets.

"You know what, macho guys? Neither one of you is going out there." Meg was putting her foot down. "I mean are you just plain crazy or what? Those men are professional killers. Put your weapons down and go talk to them. At least that way you have a chance."

Maury just looked sad. "Meggie, girl, you can't talk to this guy. There's no reasonin' wit' him. He'd nail your knees to the floor just for sneezin' too close to him."

Meg shook away that mental image but the terror remained. "Then we have to get out of here right now—" she cried, her voice cracking. "You're done packing, Maury, so grab up your luggage and let's go out the back patio doors. We can be gone before they ever know it."

"We can't go out the back, Meggie. Joey there parked The Stogie right out front where our company is."

Meg could have clobbered him hard for doing

such a stupid thing. "My God, Joe, what were you thinking?"

"Oh, I don't know. Maybe when we got here I was thinking my uncle might have been kil—"

"Wait! Brilliant idea forming," Meg announced. "We'll go out the back, sneak over to my side of the complex and take *my* car!"

"I like it." Maury looked from her to Joe to his open suitcase on the bed and then resettled his gaze on her. "That's a real good idea. Why don't you and Joey close up my bag there and go out the back door? I'll follow you to your place."

"Right," Joe said, the sarcasm in his tone as thick as molasses.

And Meg added, "Do you really think we're that stupid, Maury?"

"Look, you kids gotta let me do this. This guy don't care about nothin' but his property—"

"You mean the keys and what they go to, right?"

Maury stared, rather blankly, at his nephew. "Keys?" Then, his expression cleared. "Oh, you're talking about the wise guys from this weekend."

That didn't sound right to Meg. Then she recalled Maury had said *him* and *he* a minute ago, not *them* and *they*. *Uh-oh.* "Maury," she said slowly, "who are you talking about?"

Before Maury could answer, if indeed he'd been going to, Joe butted in. "I hate to butt in, but I figure we have about thirty seconds before we're the lead story on the evening news. So tell me, Uncle Maury— and I mean right *now*—what the heck is going on. What's all this stuff about The Stogie and these keys? You have their money, don't you? Talk fast."

Surprisingly, Maury did. "I used to have it. Anyhow, it ain't theirs. It's their grandfather's. What happened was, back in the sixties, my, uh, former associate had to go to prison—on a technicality—so he asked me to hold this wad of dough for him until he got out and could send for it—"

"That's who these guys are?" Disbelief rang in Joe's voice. "Three brothers sent down from New Jersey to take care of their grandfather's business?"

"Two of them are brothers and one's an associate of theirs—at least that's what they said through the door last Friday night. See, Freddie Ferlinetti—that's the old man—got out of the slammer. I never thought he would. I thought he'd die before that happened, the old bastard. But guess what? He didn't. And guess what else? I ain't got his dough no more."

"I've got it!" Meg released Joe in her excitement and stepped up to his side.

"You have the money?"

"No, Joe, I mean I know what Maury means. Those keys go to a bank lockbox." She turned to Maury. "Is that where the money is? In a bank? If it is, there's no way you can get it until tomorrow when they open. His grandsons will know that. Just tell them you'll go—"

"You're wrong, Meggie. I'm sorry. But it ain't in no bank. Well, it is. But not like you're thinking."

Only too aware of the continued pounding on the front door—why they hadn't broken the door down or broken out a window by now and just barged in, she'd never know, not that she wasn't glad they hadn't—she put her hands on her hips. "Then, where is it, Maury? Where's Ferlinetti's money?"

"It's all around you."

That made no sense. Meg exchanged a look with

Joe, who took up the questioning. "Uncle Maury, you still haven't told us a damn thing. And I don't know why I keep asking, but what's all this business, then, with The Stogie?"

"Oh, that. They think the money's in a lockbox in The Stogie's trunk."

"Why do they think that?"

"Because I told Freddie the Flamethrower I'd always keep it there."

"Oh dear God," Meg said, her voice rising. "I do not even want to know how that man got that nickname."

"Me, either," Joe seconded. "But, come on, Uncle Maury, there's more to it than that. All they had to do was steal The Stogie, pop the trunk and take the lockbox. Hell, I even offered the car and the keys to them yesterday when they had Meg. They didn't want it. Or her. They just let her go."

Meg nodded, corroborating his story. "They did. They just let me go."

Maury was shaking his head and looking confused. "Then I don't know what they're thinking. Maybe they're just stupid."

"They didn't strike me as stupid."

"Maybe they misunderstood what you was offerin'."

"No, they didn't."

Maury pressed his thin lips together, looking peeved. "Then I don't know. That lockbox of money is all I have of theirs."

"Had. That's all you *had* of theirs, Uncle Maury. That's why we're in this huge mess." Looking suddenly tired, Joe scrubbed a hand over his face and stared balefully at Meg. "Great," he told her. "Freakin' Mafia money. Good thing I didn't go to the cops."

He exhaled as if signaling a subject change. "All right, Uncle Maury, obviously they're not satisfied with coming to get only what their grandfather sent them after. What else could you have that they'd want?"

Maury shrugged. "Like I said, I ain't got nothin' else of theirs. I don't know what they want."

But suddenly Meg thought she knew, and the knowledge sickened her, weakening her knees. She grabbed Joe's arm. "It's him, Joe," she whimpered, looking up into Joe's face and seeing understanding dawn.

She turned to the older man. "They want you, Maury. They want the money, and you—dead. They let me go and didn't take the car because they knew we'd run right back to you. All they had to do was wait. And if you weren't here, they knew we'd find you. So they followed us until they were certain we were coming here, then let us think they'd left. Oh my God, we were so stupid. It almost worked. In another few minutes, we would have walked right out that door. But now we're trapped. What are we going to do?"

Maury smiled resignedly. It was all there in his eyes. "I think you're right, Meggie. This is about me." He looked up at Joe. "You got to let me go take care of this by myself."

"Over my dead body," Joe growled, pulling the gun around in front of him.

No, she thought. *No, not Joe and not Maury.* Before either man could stop her, Meg grabbed Joe by his head, pulled him down, planted a big, wet, smacking kiss on his lips, looked into his eyes and said, "I love you, Joe Rossi." Then she shot out of the bedroom, tearing down the hallway, running for her purse.

13

"MEG! WHAT THE HELL are you doing? Come back here!"

She didn't waste breath on answering Joe. Meg kept running, bursting into the living room, and grabbing her purse up just as someone—Joe!—grabbed her arm. He meant to stop her.

"No! I won't let you!" Meg cried out, breaking away. Terrified for him, she swung her leather purse at Joe's arm and—talk about lucky aim!—knocked the gun out of his hand, sending it flying over his head...and banging him into the wall. Looking stunned, he tripped over a potted plant, lost his balance and fell in a heap to the tiled floor.

Instinctively, Meg knew he was just dazed, but, actually, her attention was riveted on the handgun. Seemingly in slow motion, it tumbled harmlessly through the air...only to land right in Larry, Moe and Curly's tank with a wet, plopping sound. Water splashed everywhere...and the gun sank to the bottom. The startled goldfish took instant refuge in their little ceramic underwater castle. Their bugged eyes stared fearfully at Meg, who stood there stupidly staring back at them.

Suddenly, she came to herself and, like Xena, Warrior Princess, in fast motion, she ripped open her purse and pulled out her pepper spray. As she turned toward the door, her heart nearly stopped when she saw Maury already there and reaching for the dead bolt. All he had to do was turn the knob and the door would open to the murdering Mafia hit men.

"No!" Meg screamed. Maury jerked around and Meg attacked mercilessly. Using her shoulder and hip, she viciously bumped the startled old man right onto the sofa. A part of her brain registered that he landed safely on the cushions and bounced onto his belly. But the gun's stock had also hit the cushions and the weapon popped out of Maury's hands. It hit the terra-cotta tiles lengthwise and skittered away in a crazy circling motion.

Meg knew it was now or never, but she couldn't move. She stood in front of the door, close enough to touch it. Her breaths came in pants; her pulse raced. *Open the door, Meg, just do it.* Well, she'd love to, only she couldn't make her muscles work, could she? She stood frozen in place, knowing both Joe and Maury were only momentarily incapacitated. Who knew how long that would last? In the next second, either one of them could recover, grab her away from the door and stupidly put himself in harm's way, meeting those thugs with guns in their hands.

Even if—miracle of miracles—Joe and Maury prevailed, they could still get arrested. For murder. It would be worse for Maury, being in the mob, but that would make Joe his accomplice. Oh dear Lord, they'd go to prison and end up some big sweaty guys' bitches.

Meg blinked, becoming aware, in the next second, of a bigger concern. The bad guys outside had to know by now, given all the noise on this side of the door, that their quarry was trapped. Why, they could open fire at any second and hit Joe or Maury or Larry or Moe or Curly.

That did it for Meg. No one was dying today, not if she could help it. Mewling in terror, her fingers numb and clumsy, she fumbled with the dead bolt and jerked the door open. The startled men stood clustered together on the tiny front porch, staring mutely back at her. All three of them dropped their gazes to the canister in her hand. Rocco, who finally looked scared, opened his mouth to say something; but Meg cut him no slack.

Without warning, she opened fire, shrieking like she was the one being attacked, and sprayed the hell out of the three men. Screaming now themselves, clutching at their eyes and faces, they stumbled back and fell to the ground, where they rolled around, curling into protective fetal balls.

Even though they had their hands over their faces, their cries for mercy could still be heard. But Meg, still spraying, was beyond granting it. Completely panicked, she acted on pure instinct. Then, all of a sudden, her trigger finger locked. It wouldn't allow her to spray anymore. That meant her job here was done. Still terrified, not quite believing the men wouldn't reach out and grab her ankles if she turned her back—she'd seen that movie—Meg kept her canister aimed at her enemies and quickly shuffled backward into Maury's apartment.

She slammed the door, threw the dead bolt and turned around, leaning her back against the solid wood. Breathing hard, her eyes closed, she felt the canister slip from her nerveless fingers and heard it roll harmlessly across the floor. Meg feared she was going to be sick. Or would collapse. Locking her knees to keep her balance, she pressed a hand to her stomach to stem the nausea. She opened her eyes—and nearly screamed before she realized the man standing in front of her was Joe.

"I got 'em," she said.

"I know." In his hand was the soaked handgun, which he held down at his side. His gaze roved over her face. "They could have got you instead, you know, Meg."

A frightening realization, but one she could handle, at this belated point. "I never thought about that."

"I didn't think you had. By the way, this gun—" he showed her the one he held in his grip "—isn't even loaded. Neither is Uncle Maury's shotgun."

"They would have killed you both." It was a flat statement of fact.

Joe nodded. "Probably. Just so you know, that was the bravest and the most stupid act of heroism I've ever seen. But remind me never to make you mad." He smiled, but he didn't touch her, as if he knew he shouldn't—not just yet. "You said you love me, Meg."

"I do."

His blue eyes darkened. "I love you, too. Are you sure you're okay?"

Before she could reply, Maury—who was on his knees on the sofa and staring out the picture window—chortled and captured their attention. "Whew, you gave it to those guys good, Meggie! Look at 'em—like babies they are. Listen to 'em screamin'. Joey, you got to marry this girl."

Shock was receding enough that Meg could feel emotions slowly returning. Uppermost was amusement at Maury and embarrassment that he would say that. She smiled a weak, wavering smile at Joe. "No, you don't. And I'm fine, to answer your question." But in the next instant, she wasn't so sure. Something troubling hovered on the edge of her consciousness, but she couldn't quite grasp what it was.

Joe obviously picked up on this. "Meg?" Hastily, he put the handgun on a small table next to him and gripped her arm supportively. "What is it? What's wrong?"

Meg shook her head. "I don't know. Something." Fear once again gripped her. "But there's something about those men, Joe. Something not right."

Apparently, her reply faded his concern. Chuckling, he released her arm. "Hell, nothing's right with them, honey. They're criminals. These guys will be put in jail for a long time because of your actions. You just did your country a great service—"

"Oh my God, Joe, that's it!"

"What's it?"

"Putting criminals away." One hand clapped loosely over her mouth, her other planted against his chest, Meg gazed up at him in horror. "Oh, no." The something wrong had popped brightly, like a camera's flash, into her mind, leaving her feeling sick.

"Are you afraid they'll send someone after you, some sort of vendetta?"

"Oh, someone will come after me, all right. But it won't be the Mafia."

"It will be if we don't call the cops on these guys. They won't be incapacitated all that long—"

"No, Joe," Meg said plaintively, "you don't need to call the cops. What you need to do is listen. I think I just made a big, fat mistake. I think we all did."

Joe looked unconvinced. "You're still in shock, Meg, from all this—"

"No, I'm not. Listen to me." Meg grabbed a handful of his shirt. "I'm trying to tell you I don't think those poor men out there are Mafia at all."

Irritation claimed Joe's features and she let go of his shirt. "Are you kidding me? You're going to change your mind again?"

"Not exactly. Joe, I now realize that I'd never seen two of them before. The third one is the guy who did all the talking for the limo lizards. But didn't you notice how these guys, including our mobster, are dressed?"

"No, I'm sorry, but I was a little preoccupied. What difference does it make how they're dressed?"

"Oh, for God's sake, Joe, they're not the same three guys. Only one of them is. And none of them is in mob clothes."

He stared at her. "Mob clothes? You mean they're not in black? So what?"

"They're dressed in jeans and ball caps now. And they have on these dark all-weather jackets with three big gold letters on them."

Looking more confused now than irritated, Joe shook his head. "What are you talking about? Some designer logo? A brand of beer? A football team?"

She shook her head no…slowly, fatalistically.

Joe's eyes widened, some of his confidence seeming to leach out of him. "You're starting to scare me, Meg. What are the three letters?"

"Oh, Joe." Her chin trembled. "F. B. I."

THREE MORNINGS LATER, Meg woke up slowly and reached out across the satin sheets as she turned over in the huge heart-shaped bed draped in red velvet. As she knew it would, her hand met the muscled firmness of Joe's warm, nude body stretched out next to hers. Smiling, she swept her hair out of her eyes and cautiously raised up on her elbow. She didn't want to wake Joe. She wanted to stare at him while he slept. He was so beautiful. So perfect. But all she could see of him was his head and shoulders. Magnificent in their own right, yes...but not, by any stretch of the imagination, the only scenic views the man offered.

Meg smiled at his sleeping form. He was lying on his back, his legs spread, one arm flung over the side of the bed, the other over his head. She considered the light in the room, dim but sufficient. She could do this. Daintily pinching the edge of the sheet with her thumb and forefinger, she slowly lifted it up and peeked—

"Meg, we've talked about this."

Shrieking her surprise, she dropped the sheet, which billowed softly down to cover Joe again. She stared into his merry but accusing eyes. "Hi. I thought you were asleep."

"I know." He stretched mightily, like a contented cat, flinging an arm out to capture her and pull her to him.

Ablaze with happiness, she rested her head on

his bare shoulder, which he bumped up to get her attention.

"And what's the rule when I'm sleeping?"

Thoroughly enjoying herself, Meg ran her hand over his wonderful chest with its smooth, tan skin and light scattering of dark hair. "I'm not to be a pervert and check out your package when you're not awake."

"Exactly. And what's the rule when I'm awake?"

"I can do whatever I want to you anytime I want, in public or private."

He chuckled. "No, it isn't, and you know it. Instead, we can…?"

"We can both enjoy each other—" her voice took on a singsong quality "—and do whatever the other one consents to." She tapped a fingernail against his skin. "Remind me, should we ever get married, not to write our own vows. Yours would be a series of rules, all of them starting with 'Thou shalt not.'"

"Very funny." He kissed her hair.

Safe and happy, warm and content within the circle of his arms, Meg said, "Do you like it here in Las Vegas?"

He shrugged. "It's okay. I wouldn't want a steady diet of it, but it's fun for now. I'm just glad we talked Uncle Maury into flying out here instead of driving cross-country in that un-air-conditioned old jalopy of his."

"No kidding. I couldn't have come if he'd insisted on driving, what with school starting back next Monday. But can you believe Vera Warden? Who knew what a wild and crazy woman she was away from work? I was so embarrassed watching her up on stage doing a bump and grind last night with that comedian."

"Yeah, I was nowhere near drunk enough to witness that and not be scarred emotionally. But at least Uncle Maury approved."

Meg idly sketched lazy circles with her finger around Joe's nipples, first one, then the other. "Wendy was pretty shocked when I called her out in Texas to tell her everything that's happened. Wow. Mrs. Warden is not only Maury's employee but also his girlfriend. I told you those white boxers with the red hearts he packed were significant."

"I remember that." Joe shifted about as if uncomfortable—or aroused—and quickly grabbed Meg's roaming fingers. "You have to stop that…for now." He kissed each fingertip and held onto her hand. "I just wish our two favorite senior citizens—along with Larry, Moe and Curly—"

"By the way, you were so cute holding that big plastic bag of water and traumatized goldfish on your lap during the entire flight out here. You'll be a good father one day."

"Right. Anyway, I was saying I wish Uncle Maury and Vera Warden weren't in the adjoining room."

Along with Joe, Meg stared at the locked and bolted door across the room on their left.

"Too freaky," Joe added.

"All those, uh, sounds they make…I mean, how old *are* they? They go at it like two rabbits, Joe. I don't think we're keeping up."

"I'm not even going to try. I just hope I have the same kind of stamina when I get to his age."

Meg rested her chin on Joe's chest. "I don't think

you have anything to worry about in that department. Not if the last five days have been any indication, my little stud muffin. I'm just glad I'm here with you and not in prison."

"Yeah, it was kind of touch-and-go there for a while on Sunday and Monday at the police station."

"No kidding. I thought I was going to have to kiss my freedom goodbye."

"Along with your reputation. And what were you doing flipping through those mug shots? Looking for a suitable big sweaty chick?"

Meg gave his chest a playful smack. "That did not happen." Sobering, she laid her forehead on Joe's ribs. "I pepper-sprayed three FBI agents, Joe."

"Hey, they're fine. By now. I guess. Anyway, how were you to know Rocco was undercover on a sting to catch the real Ferlinetti family?"

When she raised her head, Joe lovingly smoothed her hair back from her face. She smiled her thanks. "If we'd only answered our hotel room door in Ybor City, he would have had a chance to tell us he'd slipped away from the real mobsters long enough to let us know he was with the law. Actually, he did— through the door—but we didn't believe him."

"Well, it did seem suspicious, after all. First, thugs come pounding on the door, and then a few moments later, someone knocks claiming to be a federal agent."

"It was just like a movie, wasn't it? There he was, telling the mob boss up in New Jersey that he and those actual mobsters would take care of us, when really he was trying to protect us and not get himself killed at the same time. And we kept putting him on the spot by confronting him, didn't we? Not once did he give himself away. He was really good. He even got away from those goons so he could contact Maury to get his cooperation, but the old guy kept running away or wouldn't open the door."

"Yeah, well, none of us is going to be offered a Mensa membership over our actions in this."

Meg grimaced. "Me, especially. Those poor men, Joe. They show up at Maury's to tell us what's been going on and how it's over now. And what do I do? I go screaming out the door like a crazy woman and assault three federal agents."

"Like I said, you didn't know. At least they picked up the real bad guys at the airport before they could get to Uncle Maury. And how about that old dude? Ice water in his veins. Said he didn't know why the Ferlinettis were after him, and he had no idea what money they were talking about."

"Until they granted him full immunity. Then he told them everything."

"Like I said. Ice water in his veins. The man has guts."

"I'll say. He used the mob's money to finance and build the South Tampa apartment complex where I live, Joe—and got away with it! That property is worth millions. And the little sweetheart is going to leave it all to you."

"Along with The Stogie, don't forget. Now there's a real treasure. But you know what's most embarrassing to me about this whole thing?"

Meg chuckled. "I think so. The keys?"

"Amen. It's all so obvious now."

"Yeah," Meg said, "Naming the apartment complex Bay Water Keys."

Joe burst out laughing. "God, Meg, the old man took the money, invested it in property, shredded the letter he'd signed years ago swearing to Freddie Ferlinetti that he'd keep the money for him, then went out one night in a boat by himself and threw the lockbox and keys in the sparkling waters of Tampa Bay. All the proof gone forever. I should be shocked and appalled, but I'm not. It's just too damned, I don't know, off the chart."

Grinning with him, Meg looked onto Joe's eyes. "Speaking of being shocked and appalled, Joe, I have something I want to say to you."

"All right." With great affection, he caressed her cheek and roved his gaze over her face. "What's on your mind?"

"First, since we're in a honeymoon suite in a hotel called The Sand Castle, which is much nicer than the one we tried to build last Saturday in St. Pete, and since this is Las Vegas, home of wedding chapels, and I don't like being the fake Mrs. Smith, who has no big diamond ring—"

"Are you asking me to marry you, Meg?"

She took a bolstering breath that did nothing to ease her excitedly pounding heart. "And that's not all."

"Isn't the fact that there's nothing I'd rather do than marry you enough?"

Happiness flooded Meg. "You're moving to Tampa."

"I am?"

Meg raised her eyebrows at him. "Don't start that again, Joe. Where's the property Maury wants to sign over to you now, so he and Mrs. Warden can live in sin and travel? I believe it's in Tampa. But here's a compromise. We can divide our time between Denver and Tampa. I want to keep teaching—"

"Even after our own children come along?"

Suddenly shy, she looked down. "We'll talk about that later. So maybe summers in Denver, the school year in Tampa, and alternating holidays in the snow and the tropics with our families? How's that sound?"

"Like your friend Wendy is going to be totally jealous."

"No, she won't be. She loves me." Meg frowned, biting on her bottom lip. "You're right. She'll kill me. So will my mom. And my dad and brother. And your parents and sister. Oh God, Joe, are we doing the right thing? Maybe we should wait—"

"No. It's our life, Meg. They'll all come around. And now I have something I want to say."

"That you love me?"

"No—well, yeah, I do, of course. But I was going to say I want to seal the deal with you." When Meg stuck out her hand for a handshake, Joe playfully batted it away. "Funny." Then he said in a low voice, "I want to make love to you."

Meg's eyes widened with anticipation. She slid down into the covers and raised her arms to him. "Cowboy, I love how you negotiate."

Joe rolled over on top of her and took her in his arms. "You do? Then you're really going to love how I—"

Meg cut him off by pulling his head down and covering his lips with hers. The long, slow, sensual kiss took over, causing time and place to slip away as their tongues did slow battle and their hands explored each other's bodies. Within moments, their breathing became shallow, rapid. Their gentle kneading and unhurried massaging became fevered, grasping motions. Their whispered words of love became low moans of pleasure. And their desire to enjoy this moment, to prolong it, was supplanted by the primal need to be one, to be whole.

With the earthy scent of Joe in her nostrils, with the heated feel of him atop her, and with the sight of his naked magnificence filling her vision, Meg wrapped her legs around his lean hips. "Take me, Joe. I need you now. I'll always need you like this. All my life. I love you."

Joe's intense blue eyes had darkened with desire. "I love you, too, Meg. I have since I saw the curve of your spine and the nape of your neck in that dressing room last week. We're going to be great together."

With that, he entered her, sliding easily into her softened, welcoming center. Meg sighed with contentment as all her senses coalesced in that throbbing place. Though Joe filled her, she arched her hips to take him in even more fully. Her body, impatient for the loving dance, began to move slowly, sensually. Joe met her every thrust with a powerful one of his own, until they moved in perfect concert. Giving herself over to the pleasure, Meg closed her eyes....

"Meg," Joe whispered into her ear, his rhythmic pace never slowing, "we forgot the condom."

She opened her eyes and whispered back. "We sure did. So what do you want to name this child?"

Joe chuckled. "How about Rocco? Rocco Rossi."

Meg opened her mouth to protest, but with the power and potency of his lovemaking, Joe swept away her ability to form coherent thoughts. Arms and legs wrapped around him, Meg's entire being centered on what he was doing to her—and what she was doing to him. Nothing and no one existed but her and him. And this moment. And this bed—

And that god-awful pounding on the adjoining door accompanied by Maury Seeger's grating voice.

"Hey, Joey, Meggie, you in there? Wake up! We gotta pack and get outta here right now! I just seen Big Diamond Brody downstairs in the casino, only he didn't see me. He musta followed us here from Tampa. Hey, can you guys hear me? You're awfully quiet. What's going on in there?

"Vera, honey, go around to the hall door and use that pass key I got from the front desk. See if the kids are in their room. I'll keep talkin' in case they are. Hey, you guys, remember I said I wasn't running from the Ferlinettis? I wasn't lyin'. It was Brody who called me last Sunday at home and said he was coming down from New York for his diamonds. Only, I ain't got his diamonds. They're in the lockbox at the bottom of the bay. But I got a map hidden at home that shows where I dropped the box. I just hope no fish ate the keys to it. Anyways, we gotta get back there right now and find those diamonds before he kills me and everybody in my family. That includes you and Meggie.

"Hey, Joey? Meggie? Whadda ya doin' in there?"

Are you a chocolate lover? 🖤

Try WALDORF CHOCOLATE FONDUE—
a true chocolate decadence

While many couples choose to dine out on Valentine's Day, one of the most romantic things you can do for your sweetheart is to prepare an elegant meal—right in the comfort of your own home.

Harlequin asked John Doherty, executive chef at the Waldorf-Astoria Hotel in New York City, for his recipe for seduction—the famous Waldorf Chocolate Fondue....

WALDORF CHOCOLATE FONDUE
Serves 6-8

2 cups water
½ cup corn syrup
1 cup sugar
8 oz dark bitter chocolate, chopped
1 pound cake (can be purchased in supermarket)
2–3 cups assorted berries
2 cups pineapple
½ cup peanut brittle

Bring water, corn syrup and sugar to a boil in a medium-size pot. Turn off the heat and add the chopped chocolate. Strain and pour into fondue pot. Cut cake and fruit into cubes and 1-inch pieces. Place fondue pot in the center of a serving plate, arrange cake, fruit and peanut brittle around pot. Serve with forks.

Looking for a seductive cocktail?

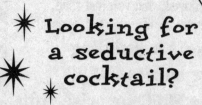

Try **Ero-Desiac**—
a dazzling martini

With its warm apricot walls yet cool atmosphere, Verlaine is quickly becoming one of New York's hottest nightspots. Verlaine created a light, subtle yet seductive martini for Harlequin: the Ero-Desiac. Sake warms the heart and soul, while jasmine and passion fruit ignite the senses....

The Ero-Desiac

Combine vodka, sake, passion fruit puree and jasmine tea. Mix and shake. Strain into a martini glass, then rest pomegranate syrup on the edge of the martini glass and drizzle the syrup down the inside of the glass.

If you enjoyed what you just read,
then we've got an offer you can't resist!

Take 2 bestselling love stories FREE!

Plus get a FREE surprise gift!

Clip this page and mail it to Harlequin Reader Service®

IN U.S.A.	IN CANADA
3010 Walden Ave.	P.O. Box 609
P.O. Box 1867	Fort Erie, Ontario
Buffalo, N.Y. 14240-1867	L2A 5X3

YES! Please send me 2 free Blaze™ novels and my free surprise gift. After receiving them, if I don't wish to receive anymore, I can return the shipping statement marked cancel. If I don't cancel, I will receive 4 brand-new novels each month, before they're available in stores! In the U.S.A., bill me at the bargain price of $3.99 plus 25¢ shipping and handling per book and applicable sales tax, if any*. In Canada, bill me at the bargain price of $4.47 plus 25¢ shipping and handling per book and applicable taxes**. That's the complete price and a savings of at least 10% off the cover prices—what a great deal! I understand that accepting the 2 free books and gift places me under no obligation ever to buy any books. I can always return a shipment and cancel at any time. Even if I never buy another book from Harlequin, the 2 free books and gift are mine to keep forever.

150 HDN DZ9K
350 HDN DZ9L

Name	(PLEASE PRINT)	
Address	Apt.#	
City	State/Prov.	Zip/Postal Code

Not valid to current Harlequin Blaze™ subscribers.

Want to try two free books from another series?
Call 1-800-873-8635 or visit www.morefreebooks.com.

* Terms and prices subject to change without notice. Sales tax applicable in N.Y.
** Canadian residents will be charged applicable provincial taxes and GST.
  All orders subject to approval. Offer limited to one per household.
  ® and ™ are registered trademarks owned and used by the trademark owner and or its licensee.

BLZ04R   ©2004 Harlequin Enterprises Limited.

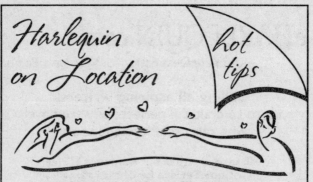

Harlequin on Location
hot tips

**Wherever your dream date location,
pick a setting and a time that won't be
interrupted by your daily responsibilities.
This is a special time together. Here are
a few hopelessly romantic settings to
inspire you—they might as well be ripped
right out of a Harlequin romance novel!**

Bad weather can be so good.

Take a walk together after a fresh snowfall or when it's just stopped raining. Pick a snowball (or a puddle) fight, and see how long it takes to get each other soaked to the bone. Then enjoy drying off in front of a fire, or perhaps surrounded by lots and lots of candles with yummy hot chocolate to warm things up.

Candlelight dinner for two…in the bedroom.

Romantic music and candles will instantly transform the place you sleep into a cozy little love nest, perfect for nibbling. Why not lay down a blanket and open a picnic basket at the foot of your bed? Or set a beautiful table with your finest dishes and glowing candles to set the mood. Either way, a little bubbly and lots of light finger foods will make this a meal to remember.

A Wild and Crazy Weeknight.

Do something unpredictable…on a weeknight straight from work. Go to an art opening, a farm-team baseball game, the local playhouse, a book signing by an author or a jazz club—anything but the humdrum blockbuster movie. There's something very romantic about being a little wild and crazy—or at least out of the ordinary—that will bring out the flirt in both of you. And you won't be able to resist thinking about each other in anticipation of your hot date…or telling everyone the day after.